YUMB

Herb Wharton was born in Cunnamulla, Queensland, and began his working life in his teenage years as a drover. His maternal grandmother was of the Kooma people; his grandfathers were Irish and English. In 1992 with the publication of his first book, *Unbranded*, he committed to novel form his experiences of people and events from his long years on the stock routes of inland Australia. His next book *Cattle Camp*, a collection of droving histories as told by Murri stockmen and women, published in 1994, has also been reprinted. *Where Ya' Been, Mate?*, a collection of his stories, followed in 1996.

He has travelled extensively throughout Australia and abroad. In 1998 he was selected for a residency at the Australia Council studio in Paris where he completed the manuscript of *Yumba Days*, his first book for young readers.

Harriet and Jonathon
Regards from Herb
I hope you enjoy this
Book

Also by Herb Wharton

Unbranded
Cattle Camp: Murri Drovers
  and Their Stories
Where Ya' Been, Mate?

YUMBA DAYS

HERB WHARTON

University of Queensland Press

First published 1999 by University of Queensland Press
Box 6042, St Lucia, Queensland 4067 Australia
Reprinted 2001

www.uqp.uq.edu.au

Typeset by University of Queensland Press
Printed in Australia by McPherson's Printing Group

Distributed in the USA and Canada by
International Specialized Book Services, Inc.,
5824 N.E. Hassalo Street, Portland, Oregon 97213–3640

Sponsored by the Queensland Office
of Arts and Cultural Development.

This project has been assisted by
the Commonwealth Government through
the Australia Council, its arts funding
and advisory body.

Cataloguing in Publication Data
National Library of Australia

Wharton, Herb, 1936– .
  Yumba days.

  I. Title.

A823.3

ISBN 0 7022 3113 4

Contents

Contents

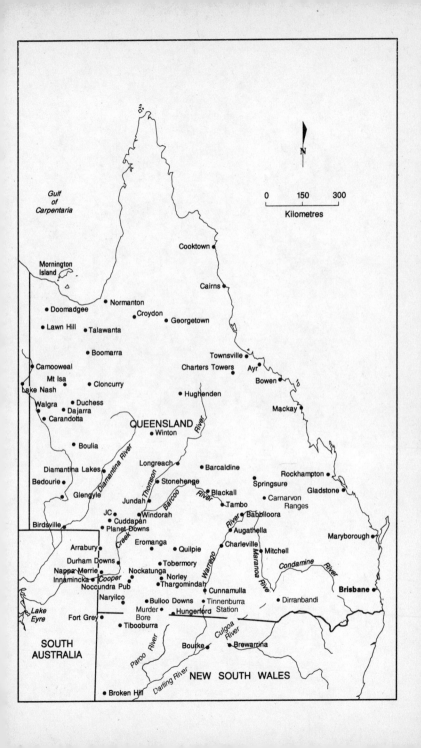

1
THE YUMBA

ONE DAY AFTER ALMOST A LIFETIME of wandering, perhaps in search of something missing from my life, I returned to the Yumba site on the outskirts of Cunnamulla. How times had changed. I became deeply moved by the silence of the place beside the cedar tree where our humpy once stood. Now, gum trees and willows were growing where tents or humpies housed the people that were so important to my past, that helped shape who I am today. Sitting there alone recalling much of what went before, sometimes with a smile, sometimes with an ache in my heart, visualising scenes from that past, recalling the sounds of voices of people long dead …

Here was part of my people's history, as well as my own childhood. The now-dead cedar tree that grew with me — planted by my parents — stood as a symbol of our history of deprivation, segregation and inequalities brought about by ignorance (call it what you may). Yet even the darkest days were always somehow overcome by hope, combined with the greatest gift of all against oppression — laughter. And education — that was my key to equality, justice, and deciding my own destiny. These things also gave me identity and strength. For if we had cried they would have been tears of blood that flooded the Warrego River.

As I grew up so did the Yumba. The local council erected more and more houses made out of used timber, and communal water taps were put in more places. Later there was the communal septic toilet, which was over a hundred yards away, convenient for those clustered around it. There were still no streets, just dirt paths leading everywhere. It took me years to find out that our address was Bourke Road, Cunnamulla. We had no house numbers and no postman, and when I came to write my first letters, replies were addressed c/o Post Office. When I asked about what address to use, the older Murries replied: "Who's gonna write to you, boy? Just put 'The Yumba, Cunnamulla' — we all know where it is."

Our house was a two-roomed shack made out of scraps of corrugated iron and bush timber, and a few cut boards, mostly pine, for the front wall. It had a tin roof and a dirt floor. Here all us kids lived together with Mum and Dad when we were small. There was a big bough-shed made of saplings and bushes to one side. Pine slabs divided the two big rooms and it had a half-enclosed veranda.

At the back of the house two square openings acted as windows. Above each window was a sheet of tin nailed only at the top, which hung down as a covering. To open the window you simply propped it up with a sapling and quickly closed it again when it rained or when there was a dust-storm coming from the west. Maybe we invented roller windows long before they used roller doors!

There was no running water; we used a communal tap a fair way from the humpy. Mum had to carry our dirty clothes over to the water tap, then slave over our big, galvanised tub that was used indoors as our bathtub. I recall one Christmas that big tub was used to make raspberry cordial because we couldn't afford to buy soft drink. When everything was washed and rinsed she would carry them wet clothes home and hang them out to dry on our front yard fence.

We used an old-fashioned pit toilet about fifty yards away. There was, of course, no electricity in the Yumba. When our old kerosene lamp was out of commission, we'd make our own from a small treacle tin filled with animal fat and with a strip of felt cut from a discarded hat as a wick. These were the days before television and computers. Yet I can honestly say that during our childhood in the Yumba we were never, never bored.

Dad was always making things for us kids. Music was something most people in the Yumba enjoyed. I was never musically-minded yet loved country and western ballads. A few families owned a windup gramophone between them and lots of scratchy 78 records. A few others had big old valve radios that were sometimes harder to listen to than them scratchy records.

Reception was bad at times. Outside the house were these high poles with aerial wire stretching between them, then another running down to the radio. When turned up loud it created mostly lots of harsh crackling static and buzzing sounds.

From a few unlighted houses would come the sound of not very well tuned guitars as would-be artists strummed, sometimes accompanied by mouth organ or piano accordion, to the beat of click-clacking spoons, sticks, or bones and the clear vibrating, piercing sound of gumleaf players. All this mingled with the night sounds of the Yumba, barking dogs or a mother's long "coo-ee" or "yhu-ay", calling kids home.

The musical sounds and songs were improvised to suit the times. So were the instruments. I once owned this unique musical instrument that Dad made for me. I still can't determine if this gadget was supposed to be a guitar or ukulele. It was created from this one gallon oil tin, a round piece cut out of one side, another hole cut in the top and bottom of the tin. A solid, flat piece of wood was placed through the holes, the ends sealed with thick roofing tar, then three strands of finest wire were used, sometimes broken guitar strings.

It was only about a quarter of the size of a regular guitar and for hours I am sure I annoyed the neighbours with some unusual, un-musical sounds. That "gitar", as we called it, did provide some food for thought and for a while I had visions of standing in front of microphones howling out the latest country music hit from some southern radio station.

Our place was always clean — not so much us boys. Mum always said it only cost a bit of soap and water to be clean. I dreaded getting ready for school, especially on Monday mornings after running wild all weekend. "I'm ready," I would proudly announce to Mum. "Come here," she would always say. "Look at your hair, it's not combed properly!"

Then she would use this big steel comb, trying to rake the knots from my thick curly hair. Next, inspecting my skinny bare legs that I'd been told to scrub under the tap, she would have me standing in a tub of water with a bar of soap. Seizing some old mattress fibre she would scrub my legs, telling me of the virtues of cleanliness and wondering what others would think if I arrived at school looking like something that had been rolling around in dirt and ashes all weekend.

Whimpering, I would submit, complaining that she would make me late. But was I really so eager to return to school after my glorious weekend of freedom with my mates?

2
THE BIGGEST PLAYGROUND IN THE WORLD

US KIDS HAD THE BIGGEST and best playground in the world, with great mates as well as enemies you could fight and talk with. The town was a kilometre north of the Yumba, hidden from view by the large white painted cemetery fence and the big red hopbush sandhill. To the south, between the sandhill and the river, was a flat expanse of coolabah flood plain. On its western side was the Warrego River. That sandhill marked the boundary of our front yard, and the river was our backyard.

We were very aware of the landscape around us, and of the Aboriginal beliefs we learned. Us kids were always learning something new from our elders, and we used the tracking skills they taught us along the dusty roads of the town as well as through the bush.

One of my mates was Jimmy Dardo, a big, friendly, easy-going boy. It seemed as if nothing could make him angry. He was something of a hero, for when we played rugby league Jimmy was the best goal kicker of all of us. He would place the ball, and I would watch, fascinated, as he raced or lumbered forward barefooted, his huge feet with the little toe of the right foot sticking straight out sideways as he kicked yet another goal.

Another mate was John, a white kid with short, straight hair. He was very talkative and argumentative — and he was the one I swapped my johnnycake with for egg and tomato sandwiches. Like me, John later became an author, and among his literary works is the biography of Gough Whit- lam, one of Australia's greatest Prime Ministers. I wonder what the odds were in them far-off days that two of us kids from that dusty outback playground would grow up to have our books published.

My best mate, Gundi, was a white kid who lived on the edge of town and spent more time with us Murries than with his own people. To me, he was one of us. His mother worked in the town as a cleaning woman. She was thin and wiry and had an acid tongue. They lived in this old, dilapi- dated wooden house with four big, high-ceilinged rooms. It was the only white house I ever entered in town, urged on by Gundi, when no one was home.

The house was more sparsely furnished than our tin humpy. I recall only an old table and a couple of rickety chairs in the living room, with drab wooden walls. But it did have tap water indoors, a septic toilet and electric light. Yet when the lights were turned on, this only highlighted the drabness of those empty, brooding rooms.

Gundi and me helped to damage that sparse furniture once, after we had seen the movie *Tarzan, King of the Jungle*, instead of our usual cowboy movies. We spent hours swing- ing from the inside rafters of the roof, yelling wild jungle calls and sometimes landing on the wobbly chairs or table. One day when we were re-enacting movie scenes we broke the chair legs and were caught red-handed by Gundi's mother. After that Gundi was forbidden to bring anyone home unless his mum was there.

I never visited his house again, but we used to meet on the sandhill to hunt and play, unconfined by walls, our imaginations unlimited. Gundi was a great thinker, but he wasn't very good at arithmetic. "What's six and six, Gundi?" someone asked him one day. Gundi thought for a while, rubbing and scratching his head and mumbling to himself, then he clasped each finger one after the other, and finally, with a lopsided smile he proclaimed loudly while half-raising his right hand as if answering the teacher: "I know, I know! That's what ya get from the headmaster when ya been real bad."

Six cuts of the cane on each hand, that was my mate Gundi's answer. A real diplomat, he always sought enlightened answers for everything.

Gundi fitted the following description — taller and a few years older than me, of tubby build, straight mousey hair, blue eyes, deeply suntanned. Sometimes there might be arguments out on the sandhill because he wasn't a Murri. "Yes, he is a Murri," I would say. "If he wants to be Murri he can be. He's our mate."

Although Gundi hated arguments or fights himself, he would sometimes encourage others to settle disputes with their fists. But if he was challenged he would protest loudly, "I can't fight! I've got this rare disease — one punch could kill me, mate. And I've got this crook heart — one hit and I'd be done for. Let's play noughts and crosses or marbles instead. I can't ever fight, true mate, real true."

We often abused Gundi verbally but we never fought him. In fact sometimes we would fight his battles for him, and then he would be our noisiest supporter, urging us on. "Give him an upper cut or straight left, mate!" he'd yell, while he shadow-boxed around in the background, throwing punches at the wind. Then, after the fight was over he'd tell you how to do better next time. That was my mate Gundi.

Horses and cattle grazed in this unfenced playground of ours — both destined to become an important part of my later life as a stockman, rodeo rider and drover, occupations which in turn would lead me to become a writer. For I have always chosen to write about the things I know best.

Us kids were certainly influenced by the cowboy movies we went to see uptown. We would jump on horses we did not own, and sometimes tumble off them again as we tried to ride them bareback. And we loved to play cowboys and Indians on that big hopbush hill, fashioning bows from the supplejack tree and arrows from the hopbush. Covered in dust and ashes, clad in our oldest shorts and no shirts we roamed the hill eating the sweet mistletoe from the wilga tree or the ripe bumbles (wild oranges).

One day as our small gang roamed the hill, we watched from amid the hopbush as a band of white kids approached across the open ground. In the lead was a kid we had never seen before, twice our size and twice as big as those who followed him. He was wearing clean pressed clothes with socks and shoes. Watching from our thick cover, this kid reminded me of a story I had heard of Moses leading his followers into the wilderness.

Spreading out, we set a trap for this Moses and his band. It was an encounter I shall never forget. When we poked our dishevelled heads of hair out of the green hopbushes, that big kid stopped as if he'd been frozen to the spot, while the others turned and fled.

Silently we stared at Moses, who stood there transfixed,

mouth agape. After a minute he screamed at the top of his voice, "My God! Wild Blacks!" Then, he too turned and fled. But he was handicapped by his cumbersome shoes on that heavy, loose sand, and was easily chased after and brought crashing down with a rugby league tackle we had learned at school a few weeks before.

Soon we were gathered around that big kid, now whimpering on the ground. We stood silently, holding our bows and arrows. The kid made no attempt to get up, but knelt upon the sand, praying: "Please God, save me from these unholy Blacks!" Imagine the effect this had on us kids from the Yumba. It was music to our ears and we went into a frenzy, dancing and chanting around him, yabbering away in devilish delight. We relapsed into English when we stopped dancing and held a pow-wow about what we were gonna do with this fella trespassing on our land.

"We could ransom him," Jimbo suggested. "Might get the price of the pictures for him. We only need ten bob for all five of us." But then we realised that none of us would dare deliver a ransom note. No picture for us tonight, no ice-cream and pies.

Hearing this, Moses seemed to calm down.

"Let's tie him to a stake," Gundi said, licking his lips.

Even though Moses was kneeling, he was still as tall as us small kids standing up. He could perhaps have given us all backhanders and sent us flying arse over head into the sand. Reaching out, I ran my hand over his thick round shoulder. "Gee, he's fat, let's eat the paleface!" I declared. That's when Moses became a blubbering idiot. Never before or since has anyone prayed like that big kid. We heaped up some dry hopbush then set it alight and flames two metres high soon leapt into the sky. I'm sure that kid had dirty trousers by this time.

But finally we decided to release him. Unlike them poor

Indians in the pictures, we had triumphed over the enemy then shown him mercy. He blessed himself then took off sobbing through the hopbush and the last we saw of him he was out on the plain, racing madly for the safety of the town as if he had a Dibble-Dibble on his tail.

Oh, how I'd like to meet that man today. I'd take him out to dinner and put fish upon his plate. I'm sure he would remember well the day when *he* was on the menu near a town called Cunnamulla, when he dared set foot upon our land.

Perhaps the fight for land rights began then, for all us Murri kids were convinced we owned that big red hopbush hill. He had taken us for wild people-eating pagans, and we were not about to enlighten him. Yet come Monday morning we would be back in school, learning more of his whitefella history, while he and most others like him ignored true Australian history.

I sometimes shudder at the antics we got up to, wandering that sandhill, and how adventure could quite easily have turned into tragedy. Like the time we came across this big red bull standing there, every now and then rubbing its long horns against the hopbush.

"Hey! He's sharpening his horns, gonna charge us!" Gundi shouted.

"Ar, he can't catch us, mate," cousin Jack said. We all knew we could outrun the horse ridden by the dairyman who also owned this bull. Sometimes, feeling thirsty, we would bail up his quietest cows and milk them. A couple of times the dairy owner caught us and came galloping after us on his chestnut pony. Off we went barefooted, dodging and weaving through the thick hopbush. The horse would labour hock-deep in the heavy, loose sand while the dairy-man, with his stockwhip cracking and cursing loudly, soon gave up the chase.

Now, as the bull stood rubbing his head among the hopbush, we decided it was indeed sharpening its horns to charge us. We watched, fascinated, and after about ten minutes decided that the bull had changed its mind. "He's not gonna charge," we decided, disappointed. Keeping a safe distance away, yelling and waving bushes, it seemed that nothing we could do would make that bull charge. "Ya gotta have something red to wave," someone declared. But we were wearing only our tattered khaki shorts. Gundi informed us that the only way that bull would charge was to start a fire. Somehow he convinced us that bulls would charge the flames of a fire, even though we knew flames were yellow, not red.

We soon had a fire going and stood around hurling insults at that red bull, daring him to charge us, but still he went on rubbing his head deep in the hopbushes. Eventually, disgusted, we decided bulls weren't that brave after all and headed home.

Mum told me to get under the tap and scrub away the dust and ashes, then she heard me boasting about this wild bull that kept sharpening its horns but was too frightened to charge us kids. "You silly boy," she said in her quiet voice. "That bull up there was dodging the flies and mosquitoes that are thick on the black soil flat with its lush green grass. Except for that hopbush, only a few tufts of dry brown wire grass and bumble bushes grow out on the sandhill — he was taking refuge."

Then she told us about this boy who lived on a station and was always sooling his pet cattle dog onto the milking cows and the bull. One evening he was asked to bring in the cows for milking. Well, he was gone for hours. Must be out playing around as usual, his parents thought. No need to worry.

Sometime later they were relieved to hear the barking cattle dog, and saw the milking cows with the bull walking in the lead, with something on its head. They thought it was a tree branch, but as the cattle came closer to the yard, the parents' relief turned into horror. They realised the object on the bull's head was their son, impaled on its horns. Grief-stricken, they had to shoot that bull to remove their son's lifeless body.

"But how did it happen?" I asked.

"Well," Mum explained, "the boy as usual sooled his dog onto the cattle. That bull charged back at the pestering dog, the dog raced behind his young master for protection, and the bull hooked viciously with its horns at the dog. The boy, catching the full force of the bull's horns, died instantly, with the dog barking frantically and the bull shaking its head, trying to free itself of the boy on its horns. The dog barked louder, sensing disaster, and herded the mob to the station cattle yards."

Even before I started school, in the evenings I would set out with my older brothers and sisters to collect dead hopbush from the sandhill for kindling, or sometimes to get green hopbush to make a broom. One such evening was my first real adventure. As the sun began to sink behind the huge Coolabah trees that lined the western bank of the river, the other kids were eager to get home, but I wanted to play on the sandhill.

"Come on, come on!" they called as they ran away dragging the hopbush gatherings.

When I still hung back, they began to shout: "Quick, here

comes the man with no head!" or "Here comes the Dibble-Dibble!" That did it. "Whaa, whaa, wait for me!" I cried, and I went dashing and dodging through the hopbush with tears running down my cheeks, yelling "I'm gonna tell on you fella!" Somehow, they always beat me home, and when I arrived with my tear-stained face, Mum would say: "What did you do to him?" — "Nothing!" they assured her, "everyone knows about the man with no head who roams that hill after dark."

Possibly there was some real basis for this mythical creature: for years some children, ignoring warnings, disappeared without trace when they stayed out late at night.

Others told of the devil dog with no head that lived on the sandhill. My cousins Jimbo and Jack often talked about this. It was always someone else who had sighted the headless apparition, of course.

One afternoon Jimbo and I, together with my cousin Jack, were out on the sandhill setting rabbit traps. We lingered there as the evening shadows lengthened. Dusk was fast approaching. Us three little barefooted kids began pondering whether we should venture into the thick hopbush among the shadows to check out our rabbit traps before it grew real dark. Might be we would run into the man or dog with no head, Jack suggested. Then Jimbo informed us in a slow, serious voice: "A dawg with no head can't bite ya." — "Hey mate, that's true!" Jack and I shouted together, regarding Jimbo with considerable respect. His enlightening us with this important fact chased away our fear for a while and we rose to venture into the murky darkness.

But Jack, who was younger than us and a lot smaller (he always reminded me of a very active fox terrier) became uneasy. He started recounting a story our Uncle Joe, a real old man who looked to be about two hundred years old, had told him about his encounter, years before, with this dog with no head.

Uncle Joe and some others had ventured onto the sand-hill one moonlit night after rain, hunting rabbits and porcupine. They had captured one rabbit and were heading home when suddenly they saw this dog with no head standing right in their path, puffing and wheezing. The hunters dropped their catch and fled. Uncle Joe, knowing he was not being chased by this ghost dog, turned and watched, fascinated, as that Dibble dog placed its neck against the rabbit and slurped it up.

Stranger still, next morning after sunrise Uncle Joe and the others went back to where they had encountered that Dibble dog. They were expert trackers, yet all they could find were their own tracks etched deep in the soft sand where they had stampeded in panic-stricken haste. No sign of a dog track: just some blood, fur and bones where that dead rabbit had fallen.

So this was no ordinary dog: it might race up to you and slurp you up through its headless neck. And it was no use throwing sticks or boomerangs or using shanghais against it, for everything went straight through its body. By the time Jack had finished telling this story, both Jimbo and I were peering uneasily into the shadows, where a slight breeze seemed to contort the swaying hopbush into strange shapes.

"I'm not frightened of that dog with no head," said Jimbo. — "Me neither, mate," I said, "but I gotta get home fast, I just heard Mum calling me." — "Yer, yer, me too," Jack added quickly, and we split and ran off to our homes.

Different families in the Yumba owned dogs and horses,

and each family would rush to protect its own dog. "We got the bestest dog in the world!" they would assert, even though to their neighbours it might be a yapping mutt, not worth feeding.

Our first dog was Rusty, given to us by people living over the other side of the hill when I was five. I went with my older brother Tiger to collect him — he was a small, reddish Pomeranian bundle and I insisted on carrying him all the way home. Rusty never grew very big but he lived a long time, some fifteen years or more. He used to race out and bark at people passing by our humpy and I'm sure he was a real nuisance to them. But to us he was part of our family, the only one that didn't get bigger as the years went by. The cedar planted by our parents grew and so did us kids, but Rusty stayed the same.

Later in life, my sister Hazel bought her own house almost in the centre of town. It was a small, low-set old house shaded by the biggest gidgee tree there ever was.

This was also the residence of Ringo, the world's worst watchdog. Ringo was a big, light-orange dog with white markings around his neck, legs and head. One ear stood pricked at all times; the other was somehow dead and flopped down limply. Maybe it did this because Ringo had been in too many dog-fights. Ringo had a stumpy tail only an inch or so long.

Whenever relations or friends came to my sister's house Ringo would race out barking and yapping, jump in the air and spin around, trying to bite his stumpy tail in sheer delight. This was his welcome for those he knew. Alas, if a stranger came to visit there would not be a whimper from Ringo. A stranger could not only enter the yard or house, but could take everything in the place and Ringo would not even bark or defend his territory.

Most of the time Ringo would sit outside the yard under

a gum tree and must have chased every car that ever drove up or down Wick Street. But poor Ringo could never catch a single car.

So one Christmas I bought four toy cars and attached them to a wire necklace and hung them around Ringo's neck. Still Ringo chased after them cars and trucks along Wick Street!

As for our first horse, I remember Dad going off to a horse sale when I was about eight or ten and leading home this tall bay mare with a busted bridle he had borrowed. Her name was Dolly. "Here's something for you to play with," he told me, "might keep ya out of trouble."

"Great! I'm gonna ride it right now," I told him.

We did not own a saddle and I remember standing alongside Dolly barefooted because I didn't own any shoes, let alone riding boots, then reaching up, taking a handful of Dolly's mane, and with one great leap finding (to my amazement) myself astride the horse. I heard Dad say, "Did you see that! Did you see how the boy mounted that horse!" But his words were soon lost as I swung Dolly's head around, expecting her to gallop off at my merest bidding … only Dolly was a dud, a jibber. That's why Dad had only paid ten bob for her: she was a carthorse that was supposed to pull a drover's wagon, but most times she would refuse to budge.

I did learn a lot about riding from Dolly, just sitting on her back, standing on top of her, and practising jumping on or off. Urging her on and riding bareback, as I realised later, made me a better horseman than if I had been taught to ride with a saddle, for it meant that I became part of the horse rather than the saddle. But Dolly did not last long; I believe she was stolen back by the person who had sold her to Dad.

After this, horses became an important part of my life; riding in the bush was soon as natural to me as walking. And horses led to a change of name for me that exists to this day. It happened when I was dawdling home after school one day — I was about six, and had just been issued with a brand-new school book. How well I recall that afternoon, resting beneath that big old coolabah tree in the gully, looking at my new book with my name printed on it: HERBERT HORSLEY WHARTON.

"Herbert Horsley," I repeated to myself, looking along the gully where two horses were grazing. Herbert wasn't such a bad name, but Horsley … gee! I shoulda been given another name instead. It sounded too much like a bloody horse. "I'm not a horse!" I thought, sitting alone in the dust under that coolabah tree. I quickly decided on a simple change; when I rose to walk home, I, *Horsley* had become *Morsley*.

Next day I had to convince my teacher that while being enrolled, someone got the spelling wrong, mishearing Mum say "Horsley" instead of "Morsley". (Mum could not read or write, so she did not realise I had changed my name.) So after that, to all the world — even to my brother's friends — I was H. M. Wharton.

Years later, when I applied for my birth certificate at the Charleville registry, I was informed there was no trace of my birth because years earlier a fire had destroyed many records. I was asked to supply some details — where I was born and my name. A short time later I received my new birth certificate, bearing the name Herbert Horsley Wharton. Yet on the electoral roll and my passport, my name is H. M. Wharton.

In time I learned the origin of the name Horsley. My great-grandfather Horsley on my dad's side came from England and married into an Aboriginal-Irish family stretching back for eight generations. (On Mum's side, my Kooma grandmother married an Irishman and bore him a dozen kids — her Australian ancestry stretches back perhaps ten thousand generations.) So without much hassle, my own slight name change can be directly traced back to them two horses grazing in the gully as I loitered home from school.

3
SCHOOLDAYS

SCHOOL IN CUNNAMULLA was something beyond the Yumba that I found an enlightening and entertaining experience, with so many other kids to play with or to fight, but sometimes I wished I didn't have to go there each day. Not being the most obedient boy in school, I was often caned for my misdeeds by the Headmaster. I would be marched into his office and out would come his array of canes and straps. Swishy, thin canes that stung the hands, thick narrow straps that made loud whacking noises yet didn't hurt like them smaller canes.

Sometimes when I was sent to the Headmaster's office, standing there while he questioned me and knowing the punishment was coming, it would actually be a great relief when he began fiddling about in his desk, deciding if it was going to be strap or cane. Of course you could never let the Headmaster know that one was better than the other, so you would plead earnestly "No, Sir, yes, Sir" and sometimes come out with OOH or AH, glad when it was over.

I took my punishment without resentment, for I knew that if you did something wrong you would be caught and punished. This didn't always keep me out of trouble, but it was an attitude instilled in us kids by caring parents and extended family members.

I had a lot of schoolmates — Jimmy Dardo, the best barefooted goal kicker amongst us, John, Billy, Col, Gundi, Jack ... to name a few. They always stuck by me, no matter what mischief I got up to.

John's father was in business in town, and John would come to school with his egg sandwiches neatly wrapped in special greaseproof paper. Mum used to wrap my johnny-cake and treacle in a used brown paper bag. John acquired a taste for johnnycake and we would often swap dinners.

Other times I would run home for dinner in the searing midday summer heat, racing barefoot over the hot, treeless ground until I reached the cemetery fence, where you could stand to take a breather, one small foot in the scant shade while the other foot rested on your knee. Then, as that foot cooled off, away you'd race over the scorching ground. I was better than most at sports, but not always the best. I played cricket and football, but running and jumping were what I did best. I often broke records getting home for lunch.

At other times Mum would bring my lunch and wait under the coolabah tree outside the school gate. Mum always emphasised how important it was to learn to read and write. Like Dad, she was continually stressing the importance of learning and getting an education. She herself could neither read nor write: I recall the first time I noticed that she used to sign papers with a cross, though later she did learn to write her name.

Dad, I believe, could have taken us all bush with him where he mostly worked, but he insisted Mum stay in the Yumba so that we would all benefit from schooling. How right they both were: learning to read and write was the

most important thing I ever did. And later I came to realise
that words were the most powerful weapons in the world.

Many of the Yumba parents, lacking any formal education themselves, had the same ideas as mine did. They
wanted us to get a better deal than they had. The adults
realised that if you couldn't add up, read or count, you were
gonna be ripped off. It was about working and wages. They
never accepted they were second rate citizens. As a result,
quite a number of the kids reared in the Yumba grew up to
achieve prominence in such fields as sport, music, literature, and education itself.

Getting back to school after lunch was sometimes a
problem. Dawdling from post to post along the cemetery
fence, gazing towards the coolabah trees that marked the
course of the Warrego River, many times I would spend the
whole afternoon down there. Bare feet cooling in the
brown muddy water, I'd check out a fishing line that had
been set, or perhaps examine a bird's nest made from mud,
which led me to wonder whether this was how adobe
building originated. You can learn a lot from nature study.

Next day at school, the teacher would ask why I had been
absent, and I would think up a number of lame excuses.
Once I told the teacher that I had thought it would be a
good idea to check out my uncle's set fishing line. "There
might be a poor catfish caught on the end and drowning."
All I got was another six cuts of the cane, and realised that
if my parents heard about it, they would give me a proper
hiding as well.

If the path to school was paved with temptations so was the
road home. Most houses we passed had orange, mandarine
and lemon trees growing in big backyards. One yard had

this huge mulberry tree that in season would be loaded with squashy, purplish fruit.

Sometimes urged on by Gundi, sometimes not, I would climb that forbidden tree, then, hidden by dense foliage, sit perched in the branches eating mulberries while Gundi stood guard. "Mate, I can't go climbing trees," he would explain. "I got this disability. Like, I could have a fit or something and fall out of the tree. Might break my leg or arm — besides, I'm heavier than you. Them branches would break under my weight, then them people in the house would come running out."

Then he'd always produce as if by magic the paper bag that had held his lunch. "Mate, when ya had enough to eat, fill this bag for me." So there I'd be perched up in that mulberry tree gorging on the fruit, then filling Gundi's bag. Then home we'd go, Gundi eating his fill of fruit.

"Where ya been?" Mum asked.

"Up on the hill playing with Gundi."

"No you haven't," she said, "you've been eating mulberries."

"No Mum, I haven't been near a mulberry tree!"

"Well, what are these purple stains all over your hands, mouth, legs and clothes?"

I was caught out and punished. "No picture show for you come Saturday," Mum said. This was the greatest punishment of all, missing them cowboy pictures, even worse than the strap or cane at school. While Gundi, having daintily eaten from the paper bag, would go home with no mulberry stains at all.

This mulberry tree was close by a great spreading pepperina, the "fighting tree", where kids would settle their disputes after school, and not far off stood the "robber's tree", where a local bank thief had been caught. Alongside the robber's tree was a big orange orchard enclosed by a

high netting fence, where us kids would sometimes steal a
few of the sweetest oranges in the world. Other fruit trees
grew there — dates and mandarines — but these huge
navel oranges were something special, something a hungry
kid would steal for. But there was one great drawback to
getting into that orchard in the daytime.

Always perched in a big gum tree in the centre of the
orchard was this big white cockatoo that screeched and
talked every time us kids emerged from the sandhill and
hopbush scrub and approached the fence. *"Missus, the boys
are at the fence!"* it would screech for all the world to hear.
Then we would go racing back to cover in the hopbush —
all except Gundi, who always acted as our lookout. (Matter
of fact, we all soon came to realise that Gundi was rarely
ever caught or punished, yet he always ate his share of them
forbidden fruits we dined on.)

Well one day, after many such aborted raids on the
orchard due to that talking cockatoo, Gundi, crouching
behind hopbush and rubbing his ample belly, suggested:
"We gotta get rid of that bloody bird or we'll all starve." So,
under his leadership, we planted our shanghais in a hole
dug in the sandhill amid thick hopbush. After school we
filled our pockets with stones, then from our hopbush cover
we declared war on that screeching cockatoo. The bird was
bound to its tree by a long chain, and as we launched our
missile attacks, that old bird would dance and squawk
around. Sometimes we'd see a white feather or two come
floating down.

We carried on our guerilla warfare against that bird until
one day, as us kids approached the high fence, no noise
came from the cockatoo. Whatever happened to that bird
I shall never know. Perhaps he had been mortally wounded
by one of our missiles. I like to believe he was released from
imprisonment and torture by the owners of the orchard.

Sometimes the past can come back to haunt you. Now I live on the very spot where those delicious oranges once grew, and the sandhill and hopbush where us kids hid is out my back door. Alas, there are no orange trees now, only berry bushes, black wattle and a few other native trees. This is where my literary career began, and many times when I'm trying to write and reach a publication deadline, my concentration is shattered by the harsh screeching and squawking of flocks of cockatoos as they perch feeding on seeds in a nearby tree outside my fence.

Quite often I venture outside to curse those bloody distracting birds. Then from a swaying branch, I imagine that one particular bird, making the loudest noise of all, is staring straight back at me, reminding me how I once stood outside a bigger, higher fence and taunted a cockatoo chained inside to a tree.

Today I am the one who is restricted in movement, since I use a cane to walk. I curse and shout, and then the bird flies off, leaving me chained to my word processor.

The school grounds were often battlefields — both mental and physical — for many kids from the Yumba. One incident I remember concerned one of my sisters.

The teacher had asked the class to write an essay relating to the interior decorations of their homes. Everyone, it seemed, had finished writing something except my sister Hazel, who sat staring at her blank piece of paper, unable to describe how one piece of galvanised iron differed from another in our shack.

So when the bell rang at 3pm signalling the end of another schoolday, Hazel rose with the others to leave but this teacher informed her that she must stay behind until she finished her assignment. The teacher pointed out that the other students had written about the colour schemes of their bathrooms, how some had green and white wash-basins or bathtubs; how some had bluish-grey lounge-room walls with fluffy lace curtains, and so on.

Well, Hazel stayed till that teacher left at 5pm without writing a word. Whether it was because of the ignorance of that teacher, or Hazel's own stubbornness, I'll never know.

It shouldn't have been difficult for Hazel to describe our place, though. She could have written about our washbasin, a badly chipped, small enamel basin on a rickety bench under the bough-shed; or our toilet, situated a hundred yards away, made of unpainted galvanised iron and smell-ing strongly of disinfectant. (If there was a colour scheme here it was ashen-brown wood always kept clean from scrub-bing by the three or four families that used it.)

Similarly, if there was decoration in our shack, it was in the many pieces of newspaper that covered the small ledge above the wood stove on which Mum stored our tins full of fat, tea, and salt. Maybe the teacher would have been really impressed by the originality of Hazel's essay if she had written one like this!

I recall one morning when I calmly announced I would take a day off school. Dad thought otherwise, "Get to school!" Stubbornly, I refused to leave and in the end I was herded to school by Dad wielding a stockwhip behind me. Yet Dad was just as determined to defend any of us against them teachers at school, several times going up and confronting them about their behaviour towards us Yumba kids.

One such confrontation had a good result for me. Dad told the Headmaster: "Okay, I send my kids to school — I've even flogged them to get them here, now don't you keep chasing them away. And all this homework — don't send it home with them. Keep them in, do what ya like, but if you can't teach them enough at school, I got plenty of work and learning for them at home. Besides, we got no light at home and they're ruining their eyes trying to see in them shadows cast by the lamp." (Many Yumba families used homemade lamps fuelled by fat — they cast more shadows than light.)

How many kids, I wonder, could tell of a father who got rid of their homework, yet who flogged them to school with a stockwhip? Yet even though Dad was what some might call a "stirrer" because he spoke up about things he thought were wrong, he never boasted of his feats.

My older cousin Nell, a big bubbly girl, went to the Catholic convent school. Her sisters and brothers were the only ones from the Yumba who attended it. One morning, as she was heading off there all spick and span, wearing her polished shoes and black-and-white uniform, I joined her as she walked over the sandhill following the path through the hopbush. I told Nell that all I could expect at school that day was the cane, having played the wag the day before.

"Oh gee, why don't you come with me to my school," she said. "We don't get the cane much there. My teacher, Sister Mary, she's such an angel, she's so soft you can con her, put on a show, cry, plead with her, and you can always get off the cane with Sister Mary, true cuz. Come on, cuz, come to my school, I'll fix it up with Sister Mary."

So with cousin Nell leading the way, we fronted up at the Convent school office to get me enrolled. What an experience that turned out to be, being grilled by these ladies covered from head to ankle in stark black and white — just like magpies, I thought. "What's your name? Where are your parents? Why do you want to come to our school?"

I told them: "Cousin Nell reckons it's better here, that's

why. I don't want to go back to State school." Then they asked me about my religion. What religion? How could I answer: "Might be Church of England, might be Protestant, might be pagan."

Well, after about half an hour, despite many interjections from cousin Nell attesting to my virtues, I was escorted back to the State school by the two biggest boys from the Convent. Much to my surprise I escaped being caned. How wonderful the world seemed again. When my mate Gundi and a few of the others learned about my attempt to join the Convent school, they became concerned. "What about sports days, mate?" John asked me. "You'd be fighting against us." — "Yer," Gundi said, "you're lucky, mate, you could have been lost forever. Them Catholics, they brand ya like horses and cattle, and make you one of their flock."

About this time I was told I should wear glasses. I did so, very reluctantly, until one day when playing cricket an argument began. "Take off your glasses ya black goanna-eating so-and-so, and fight!" a kid screamed at me, urged on by his pale-skinned friends.

Well, I did take my glasses off so I could take up his challenge, and in spite of continued pressure from my parents and the teachers, never wore them again until some fifty years later, when I began to write my books. Sometimes the pressure was really strong: one day, with all the school assembled on the parade ground, the Headmaster, who was a former State rugby union player, announced that there was amongst us one misguided student who was hampering his future by refusing to wear his glasses. And, he predicted, that student would be blind by the time he was twenty-one.

One fast bowler at school called Irish caused many

debates. He was not described as a chucker but as a pelter. He would race in making strange gurgling noises before delivering his bouncing fireballs at whoever was batting. One day it was me … alas, I was too slow in ducking, and ended up with a busted, bleeding mouth. Some kids shouted out: "Good on ya, Irish, that'll shut him up for a while!"

It did — but not for long. I ended up with a couple of stitches inside my mouth, and this meant staying home for three days, eating soup and mashed potatoes. No school! How I treasured that busted mouth, playing with our dog Rusty and no doubt making life harder for Mum. But as soon as my mouth healed it was back to school. Me and Irish are still good mates today.

In the Yumba, rounders was the most important game of all. Something like baseball played with a tennis ball, the bats were wide flat boards with handles shaped by a few strokes of an axe. Rounders was a real community game, played by everyone from toddlers to grandparents and there was no limit to the number of people in each team. People would gather when someone gave the call "Come an' have a game of rounders!" and then the selected captains, man or woman, would take turns in choosing their teams until no one except the referee was left. You could be caught out, or miss three swings at the ball, or be hit by the ball running between bases. This meant you were gone. And like the cricket at school, the Yumba rounders umpiring decisions were hotly debated.

Marbles was a very serious game and led to many disputes. Some players were noted fudgers. (This was worse than being called a chucker or thrower in cricket.) The cry would come — "Ya fudging, ya fudging!" as someone fired his marble. "No I didn't! I didn't" the accused would protest. Then all the players would offer opinions on the matter

— "Ya moved ya tor" — "No, I didn't!" — on and on it went, with all those standing around hoping to see a fight. Then, when everyone's attention was distracted from the marbles on the ground, someone would put out a bare foot, clasp a marble between the toes and walk away. When the theft was discovered, all hell would break loose with more accusations — "Ya stole me good yellow cats-eye tor!" So it went on until the bell dinged and donged, ending what was supposed to be playtime.

The annual sports day was one thing I loved about school. Not only did we compete against the Convent school, but we got free ice-cream as well. Being first in line for that ice-cream was also a sporting achievement! I made friends with two Convent boys, Colin and Noel, and sometimes after school we would get together and argue, yet those two brothers would never revert to name-calling or fighting, as so many others did.

One day after a heated debate I challenged both of them to a fight. And one of them told me: "That bare-knuckle fist fighting ain't no good for ya, mate. Bad for ya all round — broken knuckles, black eyes, even brain damage mate, the lot. Even if ya win ya lose something. But tell ya what, I'll race ya to that telegraph post ..." And this was the way we chose to decide whatever it was we were arguing about.

The greatest enjoyment of those two boys was to work with horses. Even when we were lining up for a footrace, they would be prancing around like race horses being brought into line, acting the parts of horses at the open barrier. When the word "GO!" was shouted, away we raced like the wind, barefooted along the dirt road.

Like many other kids, they ended up hanging out as

strappers at perhaps the largest racing stable in the out-back, owned by a legendary trainer. Some of these kids wanted to become jockeys, others simply to earn two bob, the price of Saturday night at the pictures.

Sometimes, when the boss was away, Colin and Noel would hold a make-believe race meeting in the feed room, amongst the bags of chaff, lucerne, oats, barley, and bran. Those boys would arrange them bags of horse fodder, and then the other kids would be told to mount the bags like race horses, while one brother acted as race caller, with vivid descriptions of the horses leaving the saddling paddock, maybe relating how one of them was playing up on the way to the barrier. While this was going on, the other brother would instruct us boys on the chaff bags how to act out the race caller's imaginative scenario. Each bag would be named after a horse in the stable.

We were always competing in the most important races, like the local cups. I realise now it was like some great play in a theatre. If Academy Awards judges had been privileged to watch the dramas enacted in that outback feed shed so long ago, we would all have been Oscar winners. Oh, how we reacted with zest to the announcer's call, making tech-nical moves, sooling horses along before the turn, trying to catch the other jockeys napping … Sometimes a fall was described, and on cue someone would go tumbling to the floor, moaning and groaning as they lay waiting for an imaginary ambulance to arrive. Close finishes were acted out realistically, whips thrashing wildly at the bags.

Then, being informed that your mount had won by a half-head, what a thrill we felt, smiling broadly and bobbing up and down as you trotted your chaff-bag horse back to the scales, sometimes raising an imaginary jockey's cap and whip as the caller described the imaginary cheering crowds. Another time you might be riding a dead 'un, not supposed to win. Because the price was too short, another lesser stable runner would be backed at longer odds, and then you'd adopt a stony-faced attitude.

Alas, the magic spell of make-believe was shattered when someone would yell, "Cocky's coming!", and panic might set in when we realised that chaff or oats from busted bags were slowly draining onto the floor, the effect of hard riding.

C. W. Easton — "Cocky", as he was affectionately called — was a Japanese prisoner of war. During the war, he helped many other prisoners to survive — many of them graziers' sons. After the war, some wanted to thank Cocky, asking: "How can we help you now, mate?" "Buy some racehorse for me to train!" was his response. So began a legendary career …

Cocky had ways of solving problems among his young helpers. One morning my mate Booty and me began arguing and shouting insults at each other at the front gate to the stables. "Hey, come back here, you two," Cocky shouted. He wanted to know why we were fighting. "We can't have ya fighting in the street," he said, "so we'd better settle this here and now." He ordered us into the big round yard and told us that we could stay there all day if we wanted, but we had to settle our argument before we left the stables, adding, "I'll sit here to make sure you do." After a few punches combined with some fast talking Booty and I shook hands and headed off to school. We're still mates to this day, me and Booty. He now lives in the city — and he owns a racehorse or two.

Cocky, unlike many other owners, did not discriminate between jockeys from the town and from the Yumba. In fact his number one jockey at that time was from the Yumba. Scobie was his nickname (after the famous white jockey Scobie Breasley) and he was an older brother of the famous Aboriginal jockey Darby McCarthy. Scobie, equally talented, had few racing opportunities.

In those days Aboriginal jockeys were not supposed to outclass white jockeys. On one occasion, Cocky took one of his best horses to contest a big race in the city. There were problems when he nominated Scobie as the jockey. "Can't have Aborigines riding here in important races," the committee told Cocky. Well, Cocky had influence and his horse did start with Scobie aboard. Cocky's horse didn't win, however.

Another incident happened closer to home at one of the many amateur races in New South Wales. An Aboriginal amateur jockey, named Bunji, was engaged for a few Cunnamulla trainers who were told by the Committee, "can't let black fellas ride here against gentlemen riders." This caused a stir amongst owners, trainers and jockeys who knew Bunji as an excellent jockey. They threatened to boycott that two day race meeting, the biggest amateur race meeting in New South Wales. Because of this stance by fair-minded white supporters that racing committee gave in. I watched with pride as Bunji rode the winner of the main race on the first day. As the racing barrier flew up to release the field that day, another racial barrier was lowered. That night, both me and Bunji were served in the pub.

Our classes at school were large, perhaps thirty or forty pupils. One day that same Headmaster walked into our classroom after we'd been given some exam results and began talking about the importance of reading, writing and arithmetic.

"Now stand up, all those who got ninety or one hundred per cent in their exams," he said. A couple of girls at the back of the class stood up, and I did too — I was sitting in the front row, before the teacher's desk. I well recall the look of incredulity on the Headmaster's face, as much as to say that I must have cheated. "Why aren't you sitting with the clever pupils at the back of the room if you're so smart?" he asked me. So my teacher explained that I was that foolish kid who refused to wear his glasses and could not see well enough from the back of the room. Besides, my teacher explained, I was not the best behaved kid in the class and needed to be kept under her eye.

My mate Jimmy Dardo had this habit of leaving his unfinished homework behind when he came to school. "Mind you bring it in tomorrow," the teacher would say, until one day she decided to send Jimmy home to fetch it. Well, Jimmy was away half the day, and when he finally came back he told the teacher: "When I got home, I had to get some firewood, fetch a bucket of water for my mum, and collect some manure — it's rained so much the mosquitoes are real bad, and we hafta keep them away with a smoke fire." All us kids in the Yumba did these jobs, but the rest of us knew that Jimmy had probably gone fishing.

I loved reading to myself, but when I was asked to read aloud to the class, I would stand there looking down at my bare, not-too-clean feet and begin mumbling.

"Speak up, speak up! I can't understand you, you're talking double Dutch!" the teacher would shout.

I remembered this when, after becoming an author, I attended a writers' festival in Amsterdam and gave a public reading from one of my books. From the back of the room a lady shouted out in English tinged with a thick Dutch accent: "Can you speak up? I can't understand a word you're saying!"

Taken aback by this statement, I stared hard at the Dutch lady, who in that instant reminded me of my teacher in Cunnamulla. "That's strange," I responded, "you know, fifty years ago I was punished by my school teacher in outback Australia, who would be forever shouting, 'we can't understand you, you're speaking Double Dutch.' Now here I am in Holland and you Dutch people can't understand a word I'm saying!"

Stranger still, a few years later I went back to Holland when my first novel, *Unbranded*, translated into Dutch, was published there. The wheel sure has turned full circle. If by chance my schoolteacher from so long ago is still around, I would love to send her a copy of the Dutch translation. I can't understand a word of it — and she would probably say: "I told you so!"

What about my other schooling, when I learned about Aboriginal history and lore at night around a campfire in the Yumba, with Aunty Ivy and Uncle Bill and others when they came in from the bush? A few of us children would sit enthralled, clustered around that small fire. It's strange, you know, when most people gather around a fire, they light a big bonfire and everyone has to stand back and yell at each other in order to be heard. But always with Aunty Ivy it was a small fire, mostly coals and ash. Occasionally she would feed another dry branch into the fire.

Sometimes us kids would play with twigs, lighting them and then whirling them around. This was something evil, Aunty Ivy would tell us, an invitation for the Dibble-Dibble to come and play. One night little cousin Jack added his own knowledge about playing with fire sticks. "Yer," he shouted, "if you play with fire at night then ya gonna pee the bed for sure!"

Aunty Ivy would tell of how you could be punished for doing wrong. Of the special power some held, to be able to turn into birds then fly away. How certain winds brought certain messages, and how the appearance of certain birds had a special significance. She told us about the Gurra-mutchas, strange, pigmy-like people who could not be seen by everyone, and who could sing you up, make you do anything they wanted. The only way to escape their magic spell was to close your eyes and avoid, at any cost, looking directly at them.

Aunty told us stories of how birds and animals got their colours, why some always flew in flocks and others alone or in pairs. Like the story of the peewees. It seemed that once there were no such birds on earth, until a man and woman from different tribes, for whom marriage was taboo, defied the law and eloped, heading into the wilderness. Tribal lawmen tracked them down, capturing them where they slept beside a small fire. Justice was harsh and swift: both were speared to death while they pleaded to the spirits for mercy. Then wood was piled high on that small fire and the bodies were cremated. The lawmen waited until the bodies had been burnt to cinders. All night that bonfire burned, then as the reddish glow of daylight crept across the sky, the bushland came alive with the sounds of living things.

The lawmen gathered closer around the last embers of the fire, now covered by white ash. Then, as the last two wisps of smoke rose up from the dying fire, just as the sun rose, they watched in amazement as those wisps of smoke, the souls of the two lovers, blackened by charcoal and whitened by ash, turned into birds and flew away. "And that's how them birds, the peewees, got their colour and why you always see them in pairs," Aunty Ivy said.

"Why were they saved?" I asked. "Why did the spirits save those bad people?"

"Oh, they wasn't saved," Aunty Ivy replied. "They was punished for ever and ever, as symbols to warn others that those who do wrong and break sacred tribal laws will be punished in strange ways."

Unlike the up-town mob, we had no electric light to read by at night. So there were no storybooks in our place. Yet there was no lack of stories told around those small fires when it was dark. Magical stories from the Dreamtime, and, when we were older, harsh tales of punishment for wrong-doing. These stories, handed down for centuries, gave me early in life the understanding that not all learning comes from books. Dreamtime learning was always combined with my education at school and the hunting and tracking skills I had learned.

When I became a drover and stockman, working in unfenced areas of the outback, and tracking straying cattle or horses, I was forever thankful to the elders who were my mentors. For these were skills not taught in schools or universities. I, and many like me, had the privilege of learning from both worlds. This is something which balances out, I think, the inequality based on colour that belonged to the era of my growing up.

4
DOWN THE RIVER

SANDY POINT, DOWN THE RIVER, was the town's main swimming hole for everyone. Shallow water, sandy river bed — even the banks were covered in sand. When they weren't swimming or diving, people used to shelter from the fierce, blazing sun under two great spreading gum trees.

Usually, we would dive from a swing in one of the trees overlooking the steep western bank. A piece of wire had been tied around a solid branch, with a piece of wood attached to the loose end. You would come running down that steep bank, grasp the handle, then launch yourself into space. At the height of your ascent, twenty or thirty feet above the water, you'd let go and then perform a graceful swallow dive, plunging into the deepest part of the river. Some would do a couple of somersaults. Others, less acrobatic, would just swing out over the water and come down feet first. (Some came plummeting down with belly flops in a great splash and had to be rescued from drowning as they struggled for breath.)

I grew up in the Yumba during the Depression days of the late 1930s in what today many would describe as utter poverty. Often we would have to heat the frying pan in which meat was cooked and dip our bread into the left-over fat because there was nothing else to put on it. Butter was something we rarely had (no refrigerator); mostly we had treacle and jam. We went without many things in the Yumba, but in other ways we were rich. Dad was a great provider for our family and we never starved.

Dad was a good fisherman. Before the days when I went to school he would take me with him and let me lie beneath a shady tree, legs splashing in the shallow water. This was great, until one day I saw this large brownish blob stuck to my leg. "Dad, Dad, a snake! He's got me, he's got me!" I screamed, dancing and stomping around in a proper corroboree. I couldn't shake this blob off my leg.

"It's not a snake, son, it's only a leech, it won't hurt you," Dad said calmly. "Might suck some blood out — sometimes that's good for you."

All I wanted was that leech off my leg. Dad said it would fall off by itself when it had sucked out enough blood, but this wasn't quick enough for me, so he removed it with the help of some salt. For a long time after that I preferred to sit on the riverbank as Dad fished.

Dad was a great bush cook. Sometimes he would cook me a small fish wrapped in mud in the ashes of a campfire, or else catch a turtle and cook it in its shell — how tasty it was, turtle soup drunk from the shell after we had eaten all the meat. Then there were always mussels or shrimps to cook on the coals.

Even back then when I was four or five years old I would question Dad about everything. Like how a bird could build such a perfect mud nest. He would respond by explaining how people the world over had learned many things from watching animals, whether it was how to build an adobe house, or how to swim, or knowing which creatures and plants are poisonous.

Creatures, he told me, were the first builders, creators and inventors. And he used to impress on me the need to work in harmony with nature, always conserving mother earth for future generations. He deplored the way people seemed to want to own the earth instead of belonging to it, being a part of it.

Not far upstream from Sandy Point, visible when the river was low, were the tops of two caves said to be the home of the Munta-gutta, the great water spirit and guardian of the waterways. Those caves were only a small part of the Munta-gutta's kingdom. Into the caves it would go to visit other rivers, using a network of underground waterways stretching to the sea. There were many stories of strange happenings around them caves. People told how, walking along the steep bank above the caves, they would see leaves and rubbish come bubbling to the surface: that was the Munta-gutta cleaning out its underground canals, a sure sign of coming floods.

I spent a lot of time down the river with Dad. He was a big, no-nonsense, practical man who had spent lots of time alone in the bush — fencing, kangaroo shooting, fishing, or whatever. He was not easily scared.

I listened, fascinated, as he told me how one evening after sundown, in total darkness, he set his gill net (a fishing net stretched between two poles) in the shallow water opposite the Munta-gutta's caves. He hurried home, and next morning before the sun rose, he returned to the river to claim his catch. But his net was not in the water where he had set it; it lay neatly rolled up on the riverbank. At first Dad thought: "Somebody's gone and taken my fish!" until he realised there were no tracks in the soft mud or sand along the riverbank. Dad was convinced it was the Munta-gutta that had removed his net, as a warning to keep away from its caves.

Other people fishing along that stretch of river would come running back to the Yumba, puffing and panting, not even stopping to roll up their fishing lines, after witnessing strange sightings like huge, partly submerged logs drifting steadily upstream against a strong wind, always in the vicinity of them caves.

Sadly, since the building of a dam across the Warrego River, the caves are now submerged. Yet who is to say that the spirit of the Munta-gutta will not return to find some way to punish those who misuse our natural resources?

Such stories were important in Aboriginal society, part of the learning process, a warning that people should not take more fish than they needed from the river and deplete its stocks. It has taken some time for our educated legislators to catch up and provide laws against the abuse of such resources.

My own childhood encounters with the Munta-gutta remain vivid in my memory. The first happened one day when Dad was away from home, working in the bush. We were short of meat and had no money left, so Mum sent me off one morning with my Uncle Baker, who was the slaughterman for the local butcher. "Give your uncle a hand then get some tripe and ginjel in return," Mum said.

With a rolled-up sugarbag under my arm, I went off to the slaughterhouse with my Uncle, past the cemetery. As we passed the school I tried to become part of Uncle's shadow, walking with him between me and the school, sure that every bloody kid and teacher would be looking out of the windows, watching me striding past. "Hey, look, there goes Herbie — he hasn't got a sore foot, he's not sick!" At the bridge we left the road and walked down the steep bank and across the wide, dry, sandy river bed, then up past a Chinese market garden to the slaughter yards.

Uncle soon set about butchering a dozen sheep and a bullock and dressing them ready for the butcher's shop, with me washing the floor and picking up scraps. Then, looking up, I saw a small, frail-looking Chinese man approach us at a sort of jog trot, two buckets dangling from wire hooks attached to a long pole across his shoulders.

He and Uncle were friends, and they chatted away until Uncle bled the bullock. The blood flowed down a drain and I watched, fascinated, as old Willie (as the Chinese man was known) placed his buckets to catch the blood before it drained away. Then, taking his pole, which had hooks on either end to hold the buckets, he bent down, hooked both buckets to the pole and rose slowly into a sort of slouch.

Old Willie looked at least a hundred, and I thought he would never be able to carry such a load. To my surprise he stood there a moment, then took off at his jog trot, never faltering or stopping until he reached his garden fence. That blood was Old Willie's fertiliser for the wonderful vegetables he grew. He lived a solitary life, catering for the township's needs, yet like us Aborigines, he was shunned by many.

Much later, I realised the contribution Willie and all the other other Chinese gardeners made towards feeding the nation.

After this, Uncle told me to wait around while he mustered some sheep for tomorrow's kill. He gave me a stern warning not to go down the river to play. "No, Uncle, I won't," I promised. After dawdling around talking to the pigs for a while, I realised they would not play with me, and it wasn't long before I decided there could be no harm in walking a few yards to the water's edge just for a look around.

Soon it became quite hot as the summer sun rose higher in the sky, so I decided to just paddle around the water's edge to cool my feet. And then, making sure no one was around, I stripped off my shorts and shirt and began to dog-paddle in the shallows until, feeling a submerged log beneath me, I perched on top of it with my knees tucked under and the water chin-high. Then I thought: "It can't be very deep here". Reaching down into the muddy water, I expected to feel the river bottom.

Imagine my astonishment when my finger tips came in contact with this cold, damp, unseen *thing*. The thought flashed through my head that it was a dead person. But no, it had a velvety, alive feeling, and what was more, I realised there were *two things* lying there side by side.

At this point it dawned on me: "It's gotta be the Munta-gutta!"

In a flash I somehow jumped off the log, turned in mid-air and racing on top of the water made for the sandy bank. Then, scooping up my clothes, I didn't stop running until I skidded to a stop behind the biggest gum tree around. Breathless, I stood facing away from the river, with my back almost glued to the tree bark, my heart pumping wildly, not daring to peek out for fear I might see a strange, monster-like head staring back at me from the water.

How long I hid there in terror I don't know, but with my breathing finally under control, I began to edge around that thick tree trunk until at last I dared to look into the water. Nothing moved. Not a ripple. No monster stared back at me. My mind was in a turmoil. Sure I had actually touched the Munta-gutta, I still felt flustered, confused. Recalling the old people's descriptions of the Munta-gutta

— I knew it was much larger than those two things I had touched. "Oh well, perhaps they were baby Munta-guttas," I reasoned.

I wandered back to the slaughterhouse, deep in thought. When Uncle came back we gathered up our bag of meat, then collected some vegetables from Willie and set off for home. Walking across the riverbed, following the water's edge, Uncle then stopped for a moment.

"Look here, see them tracks? Looks like some kid been playing in the water. The Munta-gutta musta given him a fright, he come racing out, picked up his clothes and headed for that big gum tree flat-out!"

Staring at my footprints etched deep in the sand, "Yeah," was all I could say.

"You never seen a kid down here playing?" — "No, never seen anyone, Uncle," I mumbled. He knew those were my footprints, but did not say so.

Uncle was a noted police tracker; they would call on him when people were lost in the bush. Like my Granny Mitchell's brother Joe, he could read the land as though it were some literary masterpiece that only he and others with his skill could interpret. Ever since the Dreamtime, Aboriginal trackers have been identifying people from their footprints, the same way fingerprints act as evidence today. Until the coming of the Europeans, who always wore boots and shoes, everyone went barefoot.

Yet even boots and shoes could identify the wearer. Footwear was in fact known to Aboriginal Australians for thousands of years, but was worn only by those lawmen of the clans known as Kadaitcha men — men of power and magic. (Some said that Uncle Joe had been one of these lawmen.) Kadaitcha boots were made mostly from gum wax, blood and feathers and had no toe or heel, which made it hard to tell whether the tracks were coming or going.

If the Kadaitcha man had gone barefoot, everyone would have seen his footprints and said, "Oh look, that old Joe's tracks, he's Kadaitcha man." Wearing his boots, the Kadaitcha man walked secretly on his way to cast a spell or carry out an execution of the law, just like a robber wearing gloves to mask his fingerprints.

Walking home that day, I was now deeply troubled. How could I explain to anyone what I had felt beneath the muddy surface of the Warrego River that morning? No one would believe that I knew of the sleeping place of the baby Munta-guttas. For nearly forty years I dared not share this secret with anyone, not even my closest mate, Gundi.

A few years after my strange encounter, when allowed to go fishing with the elders from the Yumba, I thought my problem was solved when we caught a big Murray cod and I felt its cold, damp side.

Another time, when about fourteen, while mustering horses down the river I heard this great splashing noise in the river. Riding over to investigate, I was amazed to see a long neck sticking out of the water, bigger than any water bird. "Oh gee, I'm looking at the Munta-gutta!" I thought. "It's heading straight for the opposite bank — I'm gonna be the first person in the whole world to see the Munta-gutta come ashore!"

Sitting there on my horse, which stood immobile, ears pricked, we both watched this strange creature swimming fast for the bank. Then I noticed another two heads and large bodies protruding from the water. I watched intently as the first creature reached the opposite side with neck outstretched, its large dark body emerging onto the bank. The magic spell was broken as this bloody great emu, water flying from its feathers, went racing madly up the bank, soon followed by the two other emus, the first I had ever seen swimming. And what great swimmers they were, as fast as any duck for sure.

My younger brothers, Owen and Robert, like me, often went bush during school holidays. By then Uncle Baker had given up his job as a slaughterman for the local butcher and started his own droving plant. They and another cousin Grace, a younger sister of cousin Nell, went on this droving trip with Uncle Baker who used to educate them about tracking, while warning them of the dangers of good and evil spirits that roamed out there.

One day after reaching camp Owen, Grace and Robert wandered off looking for bush tucker — emu eggs or whatever. Further and further away from camp they headed. Soon they became tired and paused to rest in a dry creek bed beneath a spotted gum tree. They began to eat some gum from the tree. Then they noticed this big black bull walking straight towards them!

Panic-stricken they climbed the tree and the bull walked to the foot of that tree and calmly lay down. Them kids stayed in that tree for hours cursing that black bull, sometimes throwing a branch down at it, but it would not budge no matter how much they cursed.

As they gazed out over what seemed an endless expanse of mulga scrub and red stony ridges they became afraid, wishing they had heeded Uncle Baker's and other elders' advice about dangers in the bush. Now they were stuck up a tree! They began crying, blaming each other. It seemed that black bull would never move from beneath that tree.

Back at the droving camp Uncle Baker became worried about the kids and sent one of his men, Charlie, to track them down. Following their tracks, Charlie rode up to the tree. As he did so, the black bull casually walked away, and the kids began yelling in gleeful relief.

Once they'd been taken back to the droving camp they received no sympathy from Uncle Baker, who threatened them with the strap. He told them how that was no ordinary bull, but was the spirit of some guardian ancestor stopping them from wandering further away into the dry, unfenced landscape and perhaps becoming totally lost, then dying of thirst before they could be found. Whether this was providence or chance, that black bull perhaps saved them from death. Uncle always finished by saying gruffly: "You kids will never listen, will ya."

Sometimes, on our way to school, we'd wander down the river where Aborigines who had just arrived from the bush would camp. They were mostly illiterate in English, yet fluent in their own Australian language and keepers of Aboriginal knowledge and laws. These were old people removed from the big stations that since the Dreamtime had been their ancestral homelands. I recall the dignity of such people, and how they must have grieved.

I remember one old lady who always went barefoot. Almost blind, with nowhere to live, she was offered a tent or humpy in the Yumba. She declined. However, with help from the people of the Yumba, she erected a gunya made from branches and leaves in traditional Aboriginal style.

In her old, old age, she would sometimes get us kids to gather leaves for her from certain bushes. She would burn these leaves into ashes in a tobacco tin and mix the ashes with plug tobacco. Then, for hour upon hour, she would sit immobile outside her gunya chewing on her pituri, as she called it, chanting softly in her tribal language. No doubt she was transported back to happier dreamings.

How strange it seems that in this age of drug-taking, so many rely on drugs to get high so they can forget who they really are. Whereas in the old days, Aboriginal people used drugs to induce long, lawful spells of deep meditation, of recollection. Even in the Yumba, far distant from her tribal country, that old lady was transported back to her home-land through her spiritual beliefs, now able to relive the past. For those few hours she cast her own magic spell, blotting out the forced removal from her own place.

She used the drug to remember who she really was, her Dreaming.

5
OFF TO THE PICTURE SHOW

SATURDAYS WERE SPECIAL. If Dad came in from the bush we would all go uptown, trying to outdo each other in what we were going to buy — ice-cream, chocolate, oranges, bananas ... someone would want the biggest ice-cream or bottle of lemonade in the whole world. Mouths drooling, we tagged alongside Mum and Dad, who always carried a rolled-up sugar bag under one arm. After Dad had paid the store bills we would be given some money and then we would race straight into the Greek cafe where you could buy the best and biggest slices of rainbow cake that ever existed.

The main street was always crowded, and so were the hotels. If Dad went into a hotel for a drink, us kids were never allowed to stand around near the door. We sat well away, across the street, while Dad enjoyed a drink and a chat. Sometimes he would come out with a few bottles in that now bulging sugar bag slung over his shoulder. And sometimes we would all go home in a taxi.

Saturday night was picture night. In the Yumba people would ask, "Ya going to the pictures tonight?" — "Don't know. What's on?" would be the standard reply.

"What's the name — can't remember," someone would add helpfully, "but it's two good ones, both cowboys."

Cowboys seemed the only requirement for a good picture in them days. Although many people of the Yumba could not read, posters of coming pictures would be stuck up in the shop windows, and always the ones with horses, guns and cowboys drew the most interest.

The townspeople would gather in the brightly lit main street in front of the cinema, clustered in groups on the lawn down the middle of the street. Most of the Murries would gather in darkness around the corner of the street, or in the narrow alley that led to the side entrance. Most were crowded into the cheapest, fenced-off front row seats, and often after the movie had started they would be pelted in the dark by whites sitting in the upstairs section high above the stalls.

Sometimes, as the torchlight flashed over the front rows, us Murries would be ejected from the picture house on some excuse or other, yet I never heard of anyone being asked to leave the upstairs seats. But, when the picture ended and the baddies were beaten by the goodies, everyone in the cinema cheered as one.

We kids went to the pictures on our own; Mum rarely went and I don't ever recall Dad attending. Before each session the National Anthem would be played (it was "God Save the King" in them days, and later on "God Save the Queen"). The owner of the picture house would come rushing around flashing a torch along the stalls, shouting at seated Murries: "Stand up! Stand up! Ya gotta show respect!" By the time I was a teenager, the anthem was accompanied by a picture of the Queen, mounted on her horse at the Changing of the Guard at Buckingham Palace.

Walking home, we'd debate the latest Tom Mix or Hopalong Cassidy picture. Then someone might remark: "Hey, did ya notice that beautiful palomino horse that woman was trying to ride in that funny saddle like a chair?" Or maybe — "Gee, mate, I wish I had a bridle like her horse was wearing, all polished leather and them silver ornaments."

If us boys had spent all our picture money on lollies and soft drinks, we would climb on top of the men's toilet from the alley at the side of the cinema, and there we'd lie, flat-out on the tin roof, peering at the screen through half-open windows. Our extra lollies compensated for the hard roof beneath us. During the interval we would climb down, joining the excited throng in the street discussing the action on the screen. Sometimes there would be as much action right there, as drunken fighters came staggering out of the pubs (a couple of the pubs had swing doors just like them in the picture shows). Somehow I fancy them street brawlers of Cunnamulla drank and hit a lot harder than them blokes on screen.

The picture shows were all part of our growing up in the Yumba. Afterwards we would walk home in the dark past the cemetery, discussing the show we'd just seen. We would pass the cemetery every day on the way to school or running uptown to the shops. Its high, white-painted posts were shaped like stakes and held up wire netting and barbed wire on top. The entrance was through two high iron gates about three metres wide that failed to meet in the middle, and were held together by a heavy, rusty chain fastened with a huge padlock. The ends of the chain hung down about half a metre. A white-painted lattice archway towered above the gate.

In the dark, after a Saturday night cowboy picture, it seemed quite different passing by the cemetery. If it was winter we would be wearing dark serge coats to protect us from the bitingly cold south winds. (No shoes or socks or long trousers, of course.) Sometimes, on our way home, we'd linger at the fence, like the courting couples kissing in the dark. We would creak the huge gates on their hinges, pushing them back and forth to make the chains rattle.

We convinced ourselves that by talking loudly and making a noise we were keeping the Dibble-Dibble away — for somehow we had this notion that spooks could only exist in utter silence. Of course, you could also chase them away with the smoke of certain bushes, as my grandmother had done after her son died.

Sometimes on a dark, wintry night us kids in our black serge coats would remain at the cemetery gate long after the lingering lovers, the other picture-goers and anyone else making their way back to the Yumba had passed by. Lights from the township would be reflected in the sky, while beyond the cemetery the Yumba lay in darkness. Suddenly we'd hear the sound of booted footsteps coming towards us from the hard-packed dirt road parallel to the cemetery fence. Then over the gate we'd scramble, while one of us, with his dark coat pulled over his head, would remain perched on top of the gates, like some giant headless bird, while the others lay flat-out on the ground.

As the late-night straggler drew level with us, from the gateway groaning sounds mingled with the creaking of gates on rusted hinges and the rattle of chains would be heard. We would hear those confident footsteps falter, and sometimes a loud, fearful cry — "YOUHAY!" — followed by the sound of swiftly running boots. I often wonder what would have happened if, as us kids tried to stifle our laughter, we had heard a moaning, groaning sound from a shrouded figure behind us, enquiring: "I like your style, can I join in the fun?" Us kids would have stampeded through the gate like cattle, knocking it down flat. And another story would have been born.

Us Murri kids in the Yumba were caught between two spiritual worlds, fenced in by the cemetery to the north, just a hundred yards from where we slept, the sandhill with its headless dog the same distance away on the other side, and to the west the river with the Munta-gutta, while in the Yumba itself we listened to Dreamtime myths about the Kadaitcha man. What could we do but create our own make-believe spirits?

Dad had to provide for eleven children besides Mum and himself. There was no social security system in them days. He grew vegetables in our small fenced front yard, and dug a drain with pick and shovel to the communal tap so that he could water the garden. He only used the tap late at night, when no one else wanted water.

He was also a great hunter, a crack shot with a rifle, having earned a living as a kangaroo shooter and brumby shooter when the wild brumby herds roamed the Nebine Creek area in uncontrolled numbers. We were so poor that I remember times when Dad could not afford bullets. So he would make his own, reusing the bullet shells and melting down discarded car batteries for lead. He would only buy or borrow gunpowder. Sometimes there were no bullets left at all, but that did not stop Dad. He would use traps and snares to catch his prey for food or to sell.

Most of the time Dad worked away from home. He worked many jobs, going bush to shoot or else to outlying stations, fencing, shearing, and sinking artesian bores. He also worked for the local council. One time someone working with Dad gave us kids this half-grown, injured Curlew.

Us kids rejoiced at having this unusual pet that we had often heard screaming and screeching at night but had never seen up close. Too soon, we were told by our parents, "You can't keep that bird."

"Why?" us kids shouted.

"Cause it only brings bad news."

As children we knew, yet had to be reminded, that when Curlews were heard at night around your camp it was a signal from the spirits that someone in the tribe or a close friend had died at that instant, perhaps thousands of miles away. There are many stories told of how days after Curlews visit, people receive news by Bush Telegraph confirming a death. To my great disappointment, come sundown our Curlew was set free.

When Dad was home I remember how he would spend afternoons sitting outside on the big cement block he used when he worked on motor cars — for he was also a self-taught mechanic. Sometimes, when people took their old cars uptown to the garages, they would be told: "It can't be fixed, we can't get the parts." Yet somehow Dad managed to fashion those parts from hardwood and keep the car running.

He'd sit there for hours, reading newspapers, mostly a week old, salvaged from the rubbish dump. He had opinions on everything — workers' conditions, politics, the state of the nation. Not many of the older people in the Yumba read the newspapers — or anything else, for that matter.

One time Dad applied for a job as a fireman at the local railway station, which meant he would have been with us all the time. I recall how he told Mum he had more qualifications for this job than almost anyone in town. He was determined to get it. I remember how disappointed he was on learning that someone else from uptown, less qualified, had been given that job.

In that era, many such positions were decided on colour, not intelligence or ability. I wonder what might have been if Dad had secured that job — he'd have had big wages for the first time, and maybe we could have moved uptown into a house. Who knows? Yet I doubt that Dad or Mum would have left that old humpy he had built in the Yumba.

With Dad away working, we must have been a real handful for Mum. The women of the Yumba led a hard life of never ending toil. In them days it was rare for Aboriginal women to drink — there were a few who did, but they were frowned on. Some others smoked cigarettes or a pipe, chewed tobacco, or pituri. Most people of the Yumba gambled amongst themselves, playing cards and dice, and two-up games. Gambling, it seemed, was a passion — not only as a pastime, but for monetary gain. Euchre was another skilful card game, and amongst the older men were great thinkers who did not suffer fools buying into their games.

Mum neither smoked, drank, or played cards. At night-time, she rarely went out, even to the Saturday night pictures. She was gentle, yet determined. She believed in discipline and used to punish us with a strap or a hopbush switch around our legs. And she allowed other older people in the Yumba to chastise or punish us if they caught us misbehaving. But she could be fiercely protective as well.

One act of courage I remember happened one day shortly after I had left school. The police arrived at our place to arrest one of my older brothers, who had been dobbed in by a disgruntled relative. As the two big gunghes (policemen) carried out their arrest and started to abuse him at the back of the police truck he began answering them back. They roughly pushed him into the cage, shouting insults.

Mum, half their size, walked out demanding that they show more respect and act like public servants, guardians of the law, not hooligans. The two policemen told her to get the hell out of it, but Mum stood firm, talking back to them and demanding they act properly.

As I watched this scene from Uncle's place close by, I still remember my emotions that day. I knew that the police were a law unto themselves, answerable to no one, especially not Murries. Expecting, at any moment, to see one of them gunghes give Mum a backhander for daring to criticise their tactics. I recall how I looked around for some weapon — a block of wood, iron bar, even a gun, for if they had laid a finger on Mum that day I would have raced to her side and used whatever I held in my hand to smash them gunghes down. Yet, sanity prevailed, Mum's intervention had effect and the gunghes changed their manner.

This was the first time I had seen a small, quiet, uneducated Aboriginal woman confront two policemen and win the argument.

6
AWAY FROM HOME

I HAVE A LINGERING MEMORY of my first visit to Brisbane. My brother Tiger and a few other kids from Cunnamulla, including Gundi, as well as a whole lot more from other outback areas, were chosen to stay at a hostel in Brisbane. I was about eight or nine years old. We were told it was because of eye infections — we went there for observation and to give our eyes a chance to recover. This place, the Sir Leslie Wilson Home, has since been much criticised, but to us kids back then, it was a haven!

I enjoyed my stay at the hostel — we were well fed and cared for, despite me being caned a few times. Mostly the staff were kind and the food was good. That is, except for one night at dinner.

That day a few of us boys had decided the ripe tomatoes growing next door would be great eating. We had just picked a heap of these tomatoes when we were caught and caned, told to apologise to the neighbour. As it happened, he let the hostel keep them tomatoes, and that night at dinner us boys who had stolen them had to sit at a separate table and were served thinly sliced tomatoes on dry bread, while every other kid tucked into tomato macaroni. (All them other kids gloated about us missing out but I secretly rejoiced because macaroni was the one dish I really hated. What a punishment it *would* have been for me to be included in that tomato and macaroni feast!)

Barefoot, we roamed the hostel grounds, but we had to wear our sandshoes on other occasions, like the day some of us were taken into the city on our first shopping spree. Travelling by tram — another first — us outback kids stared in awe at the size of stores like T.C. Beirne, and were amazed by the lifts inside the store, watching as people came and went from that little square box like a room. Tommie, a boy from Quilpie, watched me studying a lift then whispered in my ear: "Don't go in there, mate. See how some of them people go in as boys and come back out as girls!"

Me, Gundi, and few other country kids decided it would be safer to climb the stairs to the next level.

Those few months at that hostel in Brisbane were memorable in other ways. Like sleeping for the first time in a place with electric lights. And having a single bed with sheet and pillow all to myself in this big dormitory which held about twelve of us kids. Once those electric lights were turned off at night, all good children must be tucked up in bed. We thought the lights were turned off too early and some of us used to get out of bed and play.

Well, this dormitory floor was made of polished wood, real slippery and smooth. Most of us kids found out them pillows were the ideal things to use for getting from one end of that dormitory to the other along the aisle between the beds. We would take a short run, then dive with the pillow clasped to our stomachs and go sliding along that polished floor.

A silly sort of game it turned out to be, as a few of them kids hit their heads on the hard floor when launching themselves into the dive, but luckily no real damage was

AWAY FROM HOME 59

done. Though there were a lot of sore bums caused by this new sport: often the nurses on night duty would catch us at it, and then while the others would pretend to be asleep, us kids that were sliding would be caned on our bare bums with this long thin cane. Gee, that hurt, and we soon gave up that caper.

But that didn't stop us from trying other games. Later on, Gundi and me and a few other boys were caned when we were caught swinging, Tarzan-style, along a beam in the hostel basement that reached from the head of the stairs about thirty feet above the concrete floor, like we had done in Gundi's house in Cunnamulla.

Tiger and I were lucky. Boy, our oldest brother, was in the army at this time — for by now World War II had broken out — and sometimes came to Brisbane on leave. He would bring these great packages of lollies to the hostel, which we would gorge on until he left. Then they were taken from us by the staff and doled out to the others as well.

Boy would also take us on outings. How well I remember one such outing to the Brisbane Exhibition. There were ring events, lots of horses and cattle (which suited us fine) and fairground rides.

Yet one single incident stays with me … They were holding this sort of rodeo, and the announcer of the show begins leading this tall, rangy bay horse all saddled up into the arena, calling for someone game and skilful enough to ride this outlaw horse. (It looked real bloody tame to me.)

Soon a drunken soldier staggers out, holding a bottle of rum. He declares he can ride anything that moves. Well, the announcer holds the horse's head as the soldier mounts, then turns it loose. A couple of gentle bucks and the soldier is flat-out on his back with loud cheering from the crowd. He staggers over to his rum, takes another swig, then mounts again. The soldier has two more goes, but comes crashing to the earth both times. While he is lying there on the ground, too stunned or drunk to rise, the announcer goes on singing the praises of this great outlaw bucking horse and a sailor jumps the fence, declaring he is the best rider in the world, and that the navy can do anything better than the army.

Well, he too is a bit wobbly on his feet but manages to mount that bay after first trying to get on back to front and then from the wrong side. The horse throws him alongside the soldier, who by now is sitting up. "That was a fluke; I'm gonna have another go!" the sailor shouts. Before mounting, he grabs the soldier's bottle and takes a long swig. He lasts half a buck before crashing back to the ground.

He wants to get up again, but the soldier wants another go and another swig of rum, and so they have this great fist fight over who should ride the outlaw horse until the announcer, still holding the beast, separates them. Soldier and sailor shake hands and then the soldier grabs the horse's head while the sailor tries to pour rum down that horse's throat. Perhaps they thought that if they could get that bloody horse drunk, maybe then they could ride him.

After loud protests from the announcer, too much applause from the crowd and a couple of parting whinnies from the outlaw horse, the two would-be rodeo stars stagger arm-in-arm from the arena, swigging from what remains in the bottle. The show is over.

The tram ride; the magic box they called a lift; my first pair of leather shoes; the outlaw horse; and the pillow rides —

all were lasting experiences, yet nothing could have prepared me for my first sight of the ocean at Redcliffe. Lots of hard sand, nothing like the soft stuff back home at Sandy Point. And here there were no shady trees at the water's edge.

While most of them kids went scampering into the water, I stood gazing at the gently rolling waves as they came swooshing ashore and then receding. The ocean was a strange, whitish grey-green. People were paddling and swimming around, and further out were some small boats.

Then, to my astonishment, I saw this big blob on the skyline not so far out. Someone said it was a whale. My first visit to the ocean, and I'm not even here five minutes and I spot a whale! I didn't like to show my ignorance of such things, thinking this was something people were used to seeing all the time in their hundreds, like we do with the emus and kangaroos in the outback. Within minutes that whale was spouting water high into the air — oh, what a sight it was!

For a long time I stood alone, well back from the water's edge, taking in this strange sight, while others cavorted in the sea. Then someone called "Come on, Herb, come and have a swim, mate!" So I dawdled down to the water, still entranced by the sight of that whale blowing water into the sky. I wasn't overly impressed by the ocean, because I couldn't see where the waves came from, only where they finished up.

Standing with one foot being lapped by them gentle rolling waves, I was about to take another step and have both feet in the ocean when I saw these strange, transparent, floppy creatures close beside me, bobbing and hovering in the water like some alien life-form. *Oh gawd, what are they?* That poised left foot never touched the water upon spotting these things, which were in fact hundreds of jellyfish. I back-pedalled up onto dry sand, having got my right foot wet as far as the ankle.

For the rest of that day I stayed well clear of the water, my mates forever urging me to come and swim. Not wanting to tell anyone I was scared stiff of those repulsive alien creatures, I would mumble something like "Nar, mate, got this sore foot …"

So ended my first and only encounter with the ocean. To this day I have never swum in the sea, yet I have walked many beaches in many different countries.

For years I kept the secret of them jellyfish to myself, like them baby Munta-guttas. But about thirty years later I told my great made Gundi about them, whose only comment was: "You know, mate, you might have been a surfing champion but for them bloody jellyfish."

I have had to swim many flooded rivers with horses; I even swam a crocodile-infested tidal river once (with just a twinge of concern), and in the muddy floodwaters of the inland rivers I have had to either swim or starve. Strangely, floods and crocodiles did not deter me, but nothing would induce me to enter the sea with them jellyfish. Maybe, who knows, one day I will venture out to take just one quick swim in the surf.

One year I went to spend a holiday on the outstation about 50 kilometres from the Yumba where my sister Hazel and her husband, Bert McKellar, and their two small children were living. All around was mulga country, with hard, stony ground, and this was the setting for my first real wild horse ride — what an experience that was!

Bert had a jug-headed horse called Nugget, a sort of miniature draughthorse, which he used around the place.

I insisted on going for a ride alone. I was then about eight years old, dressed ready to ride in old school shorts and shirt, wearing a pair of discarded, worn-out riding boots and on my head a real ten-gallon cowboy hat, equally ancient. Both boots and hat, supplied by Bert, were a few sizes too big for me.

Once mounted, Nugget and I headed off into the bush, with me sometimes becoming blinded by that huge hat that kept falling down over my eyes. In fact it was so huge that it covered my entire face, and I would have to keep lifting the brim to take a quick peek ahead before it flopped back down over my eyes. Yet, no complaints; this was the greatest, riding alone wearing a real cowboy hat. What else could a kid ask for — even if for most of the time he couldn't see where he was headed?

For a while I rode with hat tilted back on my head, until a willy-willy came spinning and dancing out of the mulga, red dust swirling around, and blew my hat onto Nugget's rump. I grabbed frantically for the hat, but alas, it and my hand both struck Nugget on the rump at the same time. In a flash he took off, galloping flat-out through the trees and over the red stony ground, with me like a cork upon the ocean, sitting in the saddle trying to steer him … to no avail. Soon Nugget was racing parallel to a six-wire fence heading west. "He's gotta pull up soon," I thought desperately as spiky mulga branches threatened to tear me from the saddle.

Across a wide bore drain Nugget jumped, still following that fence. Glancing ahead I saw the paddock corner, newly erected fence wire shining in the evening sunlight. "Ah gee," I thought, "At last! Nugget gotta see that fence and stop, or else start turning." But as we neared the paddock corner Nugget neither slowed nor turned, no matter how hard I tugged on the reins. Flat-out he hit that newly completed fence and I heard the twanging of fence wires as they broke.

Without stumbling or slackening of pace he bolted through, out into the big bush paddock, still following the fence with me still on his back. Now I was starting to worry a bit as I ducked and weaved to avoid more mulga branches as the scrub became thicker. Over a fallen log Nugget leapt, then ahead, coming up fast, I saw this shallow, dry gravelly creek bed. "Gawd, I don't want to go any further with you, Nugget. I'm bailing out," I told myself as we neared the creek. "Reckon it's time to leave ya, Nugget. Ya can bolt on ya own!"

Clinging for a few yards with both feet on the off-side of the horse and gripping the saddle pommel, as Nugget galloped across that creekbed I kicked one foot free of the stirrup iron and fell to the ground, rolling and skidding and shedding one of my oversized riding boots in the process. What a relief! And no bones were broken. For a while I sat there, watching the wispy red dust trail left by Nugget as he headed into the sunset.

Strange it may seem, but at no time during that wild, uncontrolled ride was there a feeling of fear. I may not have been in charge of that bolting horse but I was in charge of my own thoughts. Only later did I realise what could have happened. Like being impaled on a dead limb of a tree. Nugget could have fallen when he crashed through the wire fence, and then rolled on me, crushing me to the stony red ground. Yet thankfully nothing had happened. No injuries, you might say.

Discovering them oversized riding boots were impossible to walk in, I slowly made my way back to the house carrying the boots, and trying to concoct some sort of story to explain why I was arriving back without the horse.

Back at the house, sure enough I was blamed for making

Nugget bolt, then told to go back and find that bloody big ten-gallon hat. I found the hat, but Nugget was gone for a few days, together with the saddle, in the wide bush paddock. A few months later, back home, I learned that Nugget often bolted — and his latest escapade was much more damaging than my wild ride.

As it happened, the horse was sometimes used to pull a two-wheeled dray when there was fencing to be done. Well, this day the dray was loaded with post wire and tools, and as the men worked along the fenceline, Nugget decided to bolt yet again. But this time, as he took off along the fenceline, the dray overturned. He kicked it to pieces, and then was gone, together with parts of the harness, for a week.

Travelling to and from the outstation for the holidays was an experience in itself. Not many people owned cars in them days, so to get there I had to ride the forty kilometres, with a makeshift saddle like an American Indian's, a few blankets strapped to my horse's back, and no stirrup irons. It was a long day's ride, and though I felt happy to be on horseback heading for the bush, I was one stiff and sore boy by the time we arrived.

Alongside the outstation there was a huge, ever-flowing artesian bore. I was fascinated how without effort the unceasing flow of perhaps a million gallons a day of almost boiling water came spurting to the surface — as it had been doing for over fifty years like some giant tap turned on without water restrictions!

This water from the bowels of mother earth was channelled into a series of drains that followed a gentle sloping incline around the ridges, carrying the water sometimes twenty or thirty kilometres, meandering through the paddocks.

It was one of my brother-in-law's jobs to see that the

drains were kept clear of fallen brush that could cause breaks so that the water would not reach the animals in the paddocks.

And that bore water had healing powers, as I discovered after my first furious ride. Stiff and sore but not sorry, I was told to take a bath and relax a hundred metres away from the borehead, where the drain had been dug deeper. Here the water was warm even in mid-winter.

Over the years, when working on stations with flowing bores, sometimes after hard falls and kicks from galloping or bucking horses, I found that bore water had healing powers often more beneficial than a handful of prescribed tablets. And that life-giving water could supply food, too, in the form of small fishes. These were said to have come up from far underground. Together with the bugglies that were thick in the paddock drains, they would often provide a feast. When the drains were cleaned with a tractor or a horse-drawn delver, you could follow behind and gather a sugarbag full of fish and bugglies to cook on the fire whenever we rested for a meal.

Besides this seafood, there were ducks and pigeons and in winter emu eggs, while other meat was plentiful, with sheep and kangaroos everywhere. Alongside the bore drain we would always find huge Mulga snakes, frill-necked lizards, goannas, in fact all the creatures of the bush came there to drink, some in daytime, some at night. Yet none came to the water around the bore head because it was too hot.

It was ten kilometres to the only mail road. This trip was taken on horseback whenever Bert expected something to arrive. Yet out here in the bush there was no feeling of being isolated, even though I had no one my own age to play with. For me it was much better than being at home and going to school … but all too soon, it seemed, after a month or so at that outstation, I eventually had to go back. Maybe it was there that the seeds of a bushman's life were sewn for me.

That was just one of my holidays in the bush. There were other times when I went off to different relations, and sometimes I went with Dad and Uncle Jim when they were erecting fences. All their work was done by hand, including cutting the fence posts with axes. Camping out was rough, although Dad could somehow provide better shelter than most and he was a great bush cook, able to make tasty dishes from meagre rations, cooking on an open fire.

During the war, Dad, like many other men, was employed for a while to work on the Charleville aerodrome, occupied by the American Air Force. Mum and all us younger kids were taken to Charleville with him, travelling there by steam train. All us kids poked our heads out the window, our eyes stinging from the cinders that flew back out of the smoking engine. We camped in two tents opposite the airfield and water was carted to big tanks shared with other families.

Charleville, I discovered, had no headless dog or Munta-gutta, but a very real menace to small kids in the form of a pet ram with huge curled horns. The ram seemed to have an insatiable hunger for bread. Almost as tall as us kids and three times heavier, it would ambush us when we were sent to the small shop on the edge of town for bread. We tried throwing rocks and swearing at that ram, but it would always run after us as we headed for home with the bread in a sugarbag dangling from our shoulders. Charging, it would sometimes force us to discard the sugarbag and then we would go bawling home empty-handed while the ram feasted.

One night soon after we had returned to the Yumba, a
few of us kids were playing together, drawing things on the
ground by the dim, flickering light of our fat lamp. As the
adults talked around the fire, that peaceful night was shattered by the loud roaring sound of a fighter plane which
came zooming out of the dark sky and flew around the town
and over the Yumba. Three times it circled low; it seemed
the pilot must be lost. After the first circuit, the elders
covered the fire and we were told to put out the fat lamp
— I don't know why, for the light was so dim you would have
to strike a match to see it.

Then, sitting there in darkness, children and adults alike
wondered what was happening. It could be a Japanese
plane, someone said — no, it must be them Yanks from
Charleville, someone else said as we all followed the progress of the circling plane. My cousin Jack said: "I don't care
where it's from, Japan, Sydney, America — I just hope it
goes back where it come from and leave the Yumba alone."
Soon after, the plane headed north towards Charleville.

Then us kids were told to rub out the crude images we
had drawn on the ground. We were told that drawing such
things on the ground at night was taboo, for the earth is
sacred.

It wasn't long after that incident that I took action against
another low-flying aircraft intruding on the Yumba air
space. This happened one Sunday while I was playing alone
beyond our front yard with my trusty shanghai, knocking
over a few tin cans. My attention was distracted by a low
droning noise that soon became a roar and I saw a plane
approaching from the south and realised it was the old-
fashioned, cumbersome mail plane making its weekly flight

from Sydney to Charleville, with a stop at Cunnamulla airfield. Watching as the plane came closer and grew larger, until with a deafening noise it was flying less than a hundred yards above the Yumba, I thought: "This bloke is showing his passengers how us wild pagan Blacks live — better give these fellas something to remember us by."

And then, as the plane flew level overhead, I fitted a stone to my shanghai and fired. Instantly I heard a loud, sharp, cracking noise like a rifle shot. My missile must have hit the propeller blade. "*Oh my God, what have I done!*"

Breathless, standing stockstill and expecting at any moment to see the plane start smoking and spinning, nose-diving downwards and crashing to the ground, I watched it fly on over the sandhill and township to the dirt airstrip beyond. Hastily, I buried my shanghai, sure that everyone in the Yumba must have heard that loud *crack* and seen me standing out in the open, but no one shouted or cursed me. Maybe for once they thought I had done the right thing, taking action against aerial intrusion.

For the rest of the day I stayed quietly at home, expecting at any moment to see that old brown police ute come racing around the cemetery fence corner, looking for the kid that had dared to fire at a Royal Mail plane. But sundown came and no policeman had arrived to take me into custody.

I relaxed with my secret, still wondering why no one had questioned me. Years later, I reasoned that the pilot did not report me because he was flying too low over the Yumba and the town. Stranger still, years after that I heard Rolf Harris sing about this old Aborigine sitting in the desert and bringing down the Flying Doctor's plane with his boomerang. Where had the idea for this song come from? Could Rolf Harris have somehow met that mail plane pilot who encountered hostilities when flying low over the Yumba in Cunnamulla?

7
GONE DROVING ...

SOMETIMES FROM THE TOP of the sandhill us kids would stand looking east across the open plain, watching the drovers with their big mobs of sheep and cattle heading south towards New South Wales, some even as far as Victoria, while others went north to equally distant places. We'd walk out and talk with the drovers in their dusty clothes, battered hats and riding boots with the heels turned over.

Walking alongside those horsemen, I would ask where they came from, where they were going, and then, as they rested on their dinner camp, I would sit enthralled as they talked about the distant towns and stations they had passed through. Telling stories of cattle rushes, bucking horses, droughts, bushfires and floods. It seemed they were always looking forward to the next stop ahead and journey's end.

Sometimes the boss would let me ride his horse to turn back some straying sheep or cattle while his drovers ate their lunch, and then for a few minutes I was someone else, no longer a schoolboy from the Yumba but a drover with a thousand miles of stock routes, two bushfires, five flooded rivers and twenty cattle rushes behind me, headed for the trucking yards or meatworks at Bourke or maybe Melbourne.

These moments were like Dreamtime stories to me. They were magical. I conjured up visions of some utopian paradise beyond the distant horizon that I would some day find, not by travelling in an aeroplane, train or car, but by riding horseback behind these vast mobs of sheep and cattle.

When my brother Fred, who was always heading off droving somewhere, returned from his travels I would not sleep in the big bed with two or three other brothers. Instead I'd sleep with Fred outside in his swag and listen as he told of rushing cattle herds and bucking horses until I fell asleep.

One day during school holidays, while I was walking home from town along the dirt road, I imagined how fabulous it would be to own a brand-new Malvern Star bike. Then, instead of walking, I could ride uptown, even offer to double a certain brown-eyed, black-haired Yumba girl wherever she wanted to go ... for to me she was someone special.

That became another of my boyhood ambitions: to own a glistening new Malvern Star bike that no other kid in the Yumba had. I never did get a bike, yet later I did date that girl, and today we are still the best of friends.

Pondering on these important things in life, just wanting that girl to share my Minties with me or sit next to me in the pictures — yet never, never hold hands or kiss (Gawd no, not that!) — I wandered slowly towards home.

Opposite the big coolabah tree in the gully, where not too many years before I had sat watching the horses graze and decided to change my name, suddenly I realised that a car was pulling up alongside me. It must be someone who was lost, I thought, someone wanting to know which way to go. Looking up, I saw this brown car, a two-seater with wide black mudguards and a canvas hood. Inside sat a man wearing a big ten-gallon hat.

"How ya goin' mate? What's ya name? You're a likely looking fella, d'you want a job?"

"What doing?" I responded, thinking he must be from some local station and never dreaming he was a drover — in my mind, drovers always rode horses.

Well, he was a drover, and had just finished six months on the road taking a mob of cattle into New South Wales. Now he was heading back to his home town, Longreach, some 800 kilometres north, and he needed someone to help drive his horses along.

"Yer, but I'll have to ask Mum."

"Okay, jump in, mate."

So down to the Yumba we went, where this drover explained to Mum what was required, and how he would look after me and send me home when the journey was finished. I pleaded with Mum to let me go, but she pointed out that I had no swag, no long trousers, no riding boots or hat. "I can fix that!" I told her, and soon I'd managed to scrounge a tattered hat three sizes too big, some well-worn blankets for a swag and a discarded pair of busted elastic-sided riding boots with heels turned over. But, no worries. I was on my way in search of something — the place where everything was bigger and better.

Bill, that boss drover, had a big old wagonette pulled by four horses. He was married to a local woman, and perhaps this was the reason why Mum allowed me to go on this journey. His wife drove the car from camp to camp while Bill drove the wagonette and I drove the loose horses. Also in the camp was this huge black pet pig that rode on the running-board of the car. Soon I was off, heading north, working for about two pounds, seven days a week. But who cares, I was on my way!

It didn't take me long to realise that my schooldays might be over, but the rest of my education was just beginning.

Each morning we caught the horses, having hobbled their front legs at night to stop them straying as we passed through sparsely fenced grazing land. I was never really homesick, because we were always heading towards some-where else. Always something to look forward to.

Arriving in Charleville, two hundred kilometres away from home was great! I had, of course, been there before. Bill, in no real hurry to get to Longreach, rested the horses in Charleville for a few weeks. And there he bought me my first pair of riding boots. "Oh, you beaut!" I thought, open-ing the box expecting to see a pair of R.M.Williams high-heeled, elastic-sided boots. Alas, they were a pair of lace-up boots that I put on with a sort of disrespect, thinking: "I'm never gonna be a real drover or stockman until I get them Williams boots."

I am often reminded of the importance of having the right sort of riding boots when I think about a great mate of mine who came to town and bought a pair of R.M.Wil-liams boots with fancy stitching. Walking out of the shop wearing these new boots, someone came up to him and began admiring them. "They look like Williams boots ya wearing, mate."

— "No bloody fear," my mate replied, "William don't own these boots, they're mine! Just bought 'em at Wiggan's store. Cost me four bloody pound."

In Charleville I met up with this other boy my own age,

whose father was a drover. We spent long days together looking after the horses, and many nights watching every picture show in town. His name was Jack. We became great mates and worked together on many jobs over the years. In later life, Jack was known all over the outback as a happy-go-lucky sort of fella who never panicked or became angry.

Yet I remember one day, soon after we first met, when we were riding along the river channels that were in low-level flood after plenty of rain. We had set out to find some straying horses. Jack was mounted on Taffy, a handsome, dappled-chestnut with silver mane and tail, his father's prized stock horse. This was strictly forbidden: Jack told me how he'd set out from home riding another horse, which he'd left with some of his father's other droving horses that were grazing around the place, swapping his mount for Taffy.

We decided to cross the shallow, frothy brown floodwater, but midway across, Jack's horse got one hoof caught up in something and began to struggle. Screaming, Jack jumped off as Taffy fell with his front leg trapped, the horse laying on his side with his head going underwater as he tried to get free. We could not help. Jack was now crying as he realised the horse could drown even in this shallow back-water. "My dad!" Jack yelled, "he'll kill me if something happens to this horse."

By now I had dismounted and was standing alongside Jack, holding Taffy's reins, hoping to keep the horse's head above water, but still powerless to do anything. Then, to our huge relief, the horse somehow freed its leg from the hidden, tangled tree roots beneath the floodwater and struggled to its feet and safety. Whew!

I had to give Jack my word of honour that I would never mention to anyone what had happened. Jack should never have been riding his father's stock horse — he would have been flogged just for that, and if Taffy had drowned, I shudder to think what might have happened to Jack. He had not earned the right to ride such a prized horse. Grown men employed by Jack's father would have been sacked for using that horse without consent, for it was a kind of unwritten law that such special horses were reserved for the job of cutting out cattle from the herd.

Taffy was his gun night horse, the most valuable partner a cattle drover could have when on nightwatch and the cattle stampeded. It was the night horse that the drover trusted on a moonless night to gallop headlong, dodging trees and hurdling fallen timber to reach the lead of the rushing herd. Then with stockwhip cracking and loud cursing, the rider would swing the leaders around back into the trailing, bawling mob. Men earned the right to ride such horses by becoming good horsemen. As yet, neither Jack nor me were in this class, even though we may have thought otherwise.

I worked with Jack many times in the years that followed — on droving trips, on fencing contracts and construction work. He became a great stockman: he did earn the right to ride special horses like Taffy. People would remark how competent and hard Jack was, yet how he was always joking. One man told me he could never imagine Jack crying.

The huge pet pig that travelled with Bill and his family was often tethered out on a chain a few hundred yards from where we camped. One evening, Bill told me to bring the pig back to camp for the night. I began to have trouble controlling that pig, trying to lead it back. It had a mind of its own, pulling me this way and that, and soon I was cursing. Then Bill yelled out: "Ride the bugger back here, jump on his back!" So with the tether coiled around its thick neck, I jumped aboard that huge pig. My feet touched the ground on both sides so I lifted and bent my legs as the pig took off like a racehorse from a starting stall. "Stick to him, mate!" Bill yelled.

What a ride! With me thinking I was in control until, a few yards from Bill's parked car, Piggy swerved sharply. I kept going, straight ahead over the pig's shoulders and head-first into the sandy ground, skidding into one of the wooden-spoked wheels of the car.

Bill and the others at the camp laughed uproariously and offered advice on the correct way to dismount from a galloping pig. Even if I'd broken a leg or an arm, that wouldn't have hurt as much as my injured pride. Me, the wannabe great stockman, wearing my first pair of new riding boots, plus my first new riding trousers! Picking some bindi-eyes from my hair, trying to find excuses for my disgraceful dismount, I looked down at my riding boots. "Gotta be these bloody lace-up boots," I thought. "One day I'm gonna buy a proper pair of elastic-sided boots, then *nothing* will throw me!"

Soon after this we departed for Longreach. The motor car, with Piggy riding in style as usual, led the way, followed by Bill driving his horse-drawn wagon and me coming behind with the horses, following the Ward River as it flowed through this vast, open country of rolling downs, so different from the terrain around Cunnamulla.

One day we met up with a sheep drover who was a few men short in his team, so Bill, whose journey home was almost finished, decided to help out by lending him me. I was to head south with the sheep drover, whose name was

Pudden, and he would send me home to Cunnamulla when he reached his destination. For half that night I sat and listened by the campfire, enthralled by the stories Bill, Pudden and others told of stock routes they had travelled with big mobs of sheep and cattle, and of their near escapes from death.

One story I listened to that night was how some drovers did not escape injury or death. Sitting around the campfire, still wearing his huge ten-gallon hat, Bill began the story, now a legend, of a cattle rush that occurred just a few kilometres from here near the town of Tambo.

It happened one night as 1500 head of cattle camped contentedly, watched by the solitary horseman on night watch. Perhaps it was a drover shaking out his blanket or a half-blind kangaroo hopping into the mob — for some unexplained reason, within the blink of an eye, the sleeping mob was rushing into the night over the campfire, scattering sparks and coals, overturning the wagonette, scattering its contents to the ground.

So unexpectedly did the cattle rush that four or five drovers sleeping soundly in their swags died where they lay, trampled beneath the rushing hooves. Their bodies were crushed into the ground, mingled with the strewn, shredded remains of their swags.

For years after, the sight was littered with the possessions of the dead drovers, amid the bones and hides of a hundred or so cattle that were too slow to rise on that fateful night. Forever after it was said that every mob of cattle that camped on that spot would rush.

As Bill finished his story, Pudden, his bare head gleaming in the firelight, claimed, "Yer, I seen the place where that occurred. It was four kilometres west of town."

"No, no," Bill interjected. "That rush took place five kilometres southeast, just out from the river bend."

"But only one man was killed," Pudden argued.

"No, mate. They was five men killed that night —" and on and on the story went, well past midnight.

Next morning I began my second droving trip, this time with five thousand sheep. I was the horse tailer, which involved seeing that the horses were well fed and watered each day, and bringing them back to camp each morning before sunrise. Pudden had only about twenty horses, all quiet and broken in. As well as these things I had to help the cook, who drove a horse-drawn wagon laden with rations and material for the sheep break (yard). The cook's name was John. He taught me a lot over the next five months and remained a great friend.

That morning, as I watched Bill head off north over the open plain, I could see the town of Tambo on the banks of the Barcoo River, that joined with the Thomson River further out to form Cooper Creek.

"That was the only place in the world," John informed me, "where it takes two rivers to make one creek." He explained that where we now stood was the watershed of two river systems, with the Barcoo sometimes flowing into the dry salt-pans of Lake Eyre and the dry inland. Once in a lifetime, he said, floodwaters reached Lake Eyre and then it became an inland sea filled with fish and bird life. Later everything perished as the waters receded, leaving a dried-up salt-pan once more, the waters heading south and flowing past Cunnamulla into the Darling River.

Oh, how many watersheds I would ride across in the years to come, crossing and re-crossing such waterways on so many outback stock routes.

Strange it was, standing there, gazing around from this treeless, blacksoil spot in Queensland, thoughts racing through my mind as I recalled the tales I'd heard the night before. Down the Cooper and further north — that's where the greatest stockmen and horsemen lived and worked, Bill had claimed.

Yet it was eastward towards the blue-grey shrouded shapes of the Carnarvon Ranges that my thoughts wandered; fascinated by the stories of wild unbranded cattle that roamed there and the great cathedral-like canyons that housed some of the oldest art galleries in the world, with rock paintings made by Aborigines thousands of years ago. Those ranges were also the hideout of the outlawed Kenneth brothers, whom I had heard men speak of with a sort of hero worship. Yet to me, listening to the tales of their misdeeds, they were murderers, criminals of the lowest order. It was like those stories about the Kelly Gang.

Ned Kelly — a criminal, or what? I recalled the tales my uncles and aunts told about Mitchell, the man who was their father, and how many had believed him to be somehow mixed up with members of the Kelly Gang. This was something that bothered me — whether it was true or false.

Over the years I have heard of many people who claimed to be the last of the Kelly Gang, as well as others who claimed the Man from Snowy River was their uncle or great-uncle, when he was in fact a figment of Banjo Paterson's imagination. But the Kelly Gang did exist, and who is to say that Mitchell, my grandfather, did not belong to it? Yet being related to an infamous criminal would not make me walk any taller. Rather, I would feel it was something I had to live down. For me, the great heroes are the freedom fighters, like the many Aboriginal warriors who fought for equality and justice: Pemulwuy and Jandamarra who were branded for too long as murdering criminals.

As always through my life, when one journey ends another

begins. On this droving trip with five thousand sheep, not only did I drive the horses but I had to gather wood for the cook, help to erect the big rope yard for the sheep, and fetch water from the creek after we delivered that mob of sheep. Pudden went mustering awhile on one of the stations.

Soon John and me headed off with the wagon and horses to another station halfway between Charleville and Quilpie, on the banks of the Paroo River, where Pudden caught up with us a little later. It was mostly red, stony mulga scrub country, sparsely watered. One of the station paddocks was a hundred thousand acres in size. The nearest neighbour was twenty kilometres away at the local railway siding, where there was a general store and a few railway fettlers' houses. I loved going to collect the mail with the boss, when I'd spend up big on lollies and soft drinks with money deducted from my wages.

I shall never forget one strange incident from that time. It was Easter and Pudden, John and me were camped in the station's stockmen's quarters not far from the homestead. Quite often I would go off fishing, catching big yellowbelly. Holidays and overtime meant little in them days. But since it was Easter, Pudden decided we must have fish for Good Friday, so he suggested I should go off by myself and catch some on the Thursday night. I think he and John wanted to get rid of me so that they could have a big booze up and they didn't want me hanging around. Too many secrets came out when the alcohol went in.

So after supper I headed off on foot to level, open ground on the other side of the river. With a billy-can, blanket, food, the lot. "Stay out all night," they'd said, "catch plenty of fish, come home in the morning." That night the moon was full, sometimes hidden by fleecy white cloud. I soon had a fire going, and after catching a couple of fish I lay resting on my blanket, gazing upward and noting how it was the moon which seemed to be moving rapidly across the sky, rather than them drifting clouds.

The next instant the sky changed. Soft, dimmed moonlight and scattered fleecy cloud became illuminated by a wondrous greenish glow caused by this object I saw silently hurtling across the sky from east to west. Not only the sky but the landscape itself became shrouded in this strange greenish glow. Every tree and hill was as plainly visible as in daylight. "Wow!" I thought, springing to my feet and wondering if anyone else was witnessing this miracle. As that green ball of light reached the horizon and disappeared, I heard this muffled rumble and felt a slight tremor beneath my feet.

Within a few seconds of that tremor, every cloud had cleared from the sky as if by magic and the land was bathed in this wondrous greenish-bronze light that was soon replaced by a soft yellowish glow cast by the full moon. Stranger still was the serenity that had descended over the landscape. And the silence: not eerie but somehow peaceful. There was no sound of bird or animal, no wind rustling through the trees. Even the river surface was calm; I saw no sign of jumping shrimps or fish.

"Bugger this!" I thought, "something real strange has happened." Not overly afraid but eager to question others about what I had seen and felt, I hurried back to the stockmen's quarters. "Did you see that thing in the sky!" I began yelling before I reached the veranda. All I heard in reply were loud snores from Pudden and John, both sound asleep, flaked out on the veranda floor alongside an upturned waterbag and a couple of empty rum bottles.

For the rest of the night I had to suffer the harsh, grating snores of my workmates as I lay wondering in the dark, "was it a meteorite? a UFO? or what?"

The unexplained fascinates me, especially when it's close to home. There is nothing more terrifying to a drover than the eerie sound that signals a cattle rush. Like a death knock, I have heard it when I have been on night watch riding around a large mob of contented sleeping cattle and there is suddenly a sound, a loud click (possibly the simultaneous click of 1000 head of cattles' leg joints) as they all jump to their feet as one panicking mass of hooves and horns.

As the rush begins the drover has no time to be frightened but instead responds to the urgent need to get to the front and turn the leaders around back into the trailing mob. What causes these rushes I would often ponder. Sometimes reasons could be found. Other times it would seem that the only logical cause of a cattle rush was that the sleeping cattle all had a nightmare at the same time. Perhaps of some bearded, red-eyed, illuminated Dibble-Dibble drover wielding a flashing electric stockwhip, coming at them at full gallop. After all, I have seen cattle flatten fences and yards, rushing for no apparent reason.

One moonlit night as we camped cattle in the corner of two fences, just off a rarely used dirt road not far outside a small, one pub town, I was amazed to hear the sound of someone merrily (but not very tunefully) singing a song about open sky, open road. Coming towards me from the direction of town, out of the shadowy trees into the moonlight, appeared this man on a pushbike. Slightly intoxicated, he had lost track of the faintly marked road and was pedalling across open ground directly towards the sleeping cattle.

"Oh gawd. This bloody idiot is gonna cause the biggest cattle rush in history," I thought. So I went up to him on the night horse, calling out, "Stop, Stop! Ya off the bloody road! Git back over there! Ya heading into a mob of sleeping cattle!"

"La-da-da hey, hey, hey," he chanted, merrily waving one arm as a form of greeting to me and the night horse. That pushbike cowboy never had a worry in the world. The bike wobbled and I wished he would fall but he pedalled on.

As I watched in horror the bike headed for a young steer that lay sleeping a few metres from the mob. With a metallic *bang* — the cowboy flew off his bike and over the back of the sleeping steer and nose-dived into the ground.

"Where am I? Where am I?" he repeated as he sat up.

He sat there beside the sleeping herd as the steer, loath to leave a good sleeping spot, rose reluctantly to its feet and joined its mob.

"What the bloody hell ya doing out here riding around drunk at night?" I demanded, still shaking from the anticipated rush.

"Oh, on my way home," the dazed cowboy replied. "Where am I?"

"Well," I answered in a low voice, straining to keep the peace, "you're sitting in the claypan on Wyandra Common alongside 1200 head of cattle that ya almost caused to rush."

By the time I helped him to remount and steered him in the right direction home, my humour had returned and I had a laugh — a quiet one though, so as not to disturb the mob.

Banjo, the station night horse, continued my other education. Every morning as dawn was breaking it was my task to muster the horses that roamed free in the big horse paddock, with only the sound of a couple of horse-bells to reveal where they were. From the mulga scrub I would muster them into the horse yard for an early morning start.

This was different to when we were droving, when the horses were hobbled out.

By day, Banjo ran loose in a small paddock and at night he was stabled. He was an intelligent horse, a bay pony about twelve hands and hard to turn. Sometimes, when I went to get him, I would spend hours trying to catch him. Until one day Jack said: "Boy, ya never gonna catch that horse walking out there with a bridle in ya hands." So I had to outwit Banjo somehow.

Quite often he would be a kilometre away from the station yards. I decided to get smart by carrying a long piece of thick twine in my trousers pocket instead of a bridle, and with arms swinging would head off in search of Banjo. He would see me coming, then stand with neck arched, ears pricked, eyes wide open, no doubt noting my progress … with no bridle in sight. I would be calling out to him, telling him what a wonderful pony he was: "Gidday, Banjo, you're the bestus little horse in the world!"

Soon I was standing alongside him, rubbing his neck and ears, talking all the time while I removed the twine from my pocket and slipped it around his neck. Then, with a couple of loops over his nose I would lead him to the yards with my bush halter.

One day I decided it was too far to walk back to the yards, so I vaulted onto Banjo's back, sure I would be able to control him without a bridle, using only my makeshift twine halter. But he took off flat-out, galloping towards the horse yards through the mulga with me crouched along his neck dodging tree branches. Banjo didn't stop as he reached the yard's open gate. Straight through he galloped, almost crushing my foot against the huge gatepost. But I clung on.

At last he stopped and I slid from his back in agony: my injured foot was turning blue when I removed my riding boot. I hobbled back to the stockmen's quarters, where I spent the next few days swallowing Bex powders and resting until I could ride again.

Shortly after this I was sacked. Nothing to do with how I did my work but because of my incurable habit of asking questions.

"Ya sacked!" Pudden screamed one day when I had asked one question too many.

After five months' work I got little pay — musta spent it all on lollies and lemonade at the railway siding. Anyway, I had a few pounds in my pocket, and I hitched a ride to Charleville, where I bought myself my first pair of elastic-sided riding boots, then took the train home to Cunnamulla.

I remember how my younger brothers and cousins followed me uptown from the Yumba, whining for chocolate, soft drinks and fruit and the cowboy pictures. I had to tell them I was broke, that I had no bungo. All the same, I felt like a king with empty pockets as I recounted my first real horseback adventures, which had lasted about six months.

So that was my first experience of droving. Eagerly I looked forward to the next.

Back in the Yumba, us louts, or "half-axes", as young people out of work were called in them days, created our own amusement, fishing or swimming in the river. There were a few Aborigines with droving plants living in the Yumba, and they would sometimes offer us work. When we weren't droving a few of us worked at the racing stables as strappers. Horses were never too far away.

In them droving days, arguing with the boss and being sacked was part of the learning process. Sometimes you'd tell the boss you were leaving before he told you to go. Like on one cold night not far from Cunnamulla, when I was working for another drover. There were only the two of us, with about a hundred head of cattle and some horses. This night we camped with the cattle bedded down in the corner of two fences with a few fires lit; all we had to do was keep the fires alight or mount the night horse to turn back any cattle that strayed. But about two in the morning, them cattle were suddenly awake and stampeding into the night.

Before I could mount the night horse, that boss drover came rushing up to me, stockwhip in hand, shouting: "Ya made them cattle rush! Ya made them rush!" and he began to belt me with his stockwhip. How could I possibly have made them cattle rush?

"Now get them other horses so we can muster them bloody cattle before I sack ya!" he shouted.

"Sack me then, ya bastard!" I yelled, letting go of the night horse's reins and letting him trot off — "get ya own horses, muster ya own cattle!"

Then, as that enraged boss went scurrying into the darkness after his night horse, I rolled up my swag and walked away into the night. I would have been about fifteen at the time.

Being sacked in them days was no great disgrace. Sometimes it was a real honour. And no job was really permanent. The tale was told of this stockman on one of the largest stations in the south-west who was informed they could no longer afford him after forty-five years of loyal service. I'm told that was the only time anyone ever heard that old stockman swear. When the station manager gave him the devastating news, he shouted: "Ya slimy marsupial! If I'd a'known this bloody job wasn't permanent I wouldn't have come here to work in the first place!"

Yet there were many good bosses that far outweighed the

bad ones. I had a fair number of disputes with bosses over the years, yet remained mates with most of them. Even the boss drover I fought with on a lonely stock route in outback Queensland. We went at it in true Saltbush Bill, bare-knuckle style, watched by twelve hundred cattle, fifty horses, six dogs and a couple of other drovers. That boss, realising he was losing the fight, began calling out to his loyal blue cattle dog: "Here, Blue, here, come and bite this bastard! Bite him, Blue!"

Well, out from beneath the old wagonette, like a streak of lightning, came old Blue. As the boss grabbed me in a clinch, Blue, with teeth bared and lips curled back, snarling for all he was worth, leapt to his master's aid. As we swung around, old Blue took one hard bite and a piece of meat out of his *master's* backside. In disbelief the boss broke away and started dancing around, both hands clasped to his backside, yelling: "My bloody dog, he bit a piece outa me arse!"

By this time my fury turned into laughter as I watched his antics. He pranced around on that vast open plain cursing not only unfaithful dogs but cheeky stockmen as well. But he would not sack me even after that fight, and I being well fed and paid, would not leave. Me and that boss drover are still friends, despite that day when old Blue bit a piece out of the arse belonging to the hand that fed him.

8
... OFF TO BOURKE

BY NOW I WAS FIFTEEN and getting man's wages as a stock-man, like brother Fred, and that meant working as soon as a job became available, wherever, whenever. One day I was asked to take twelve horses from a station near Cunnamulla to Bourke, in New South Wales.

I collected them horses and started off along the track, my swag and provisions carried by a pack horse: meagre rations of one loaf of bread, tea, sugar, salt, a tin of treacle, a few tins of meat, a couple of potatoes and onions, a packet of self-raising flour to make damper along the way, and some fresh chops from the station boss.

A condamine bell dangled and donged from the pack horse's neck, and each of the other horses had hobbles strapped around their necks. Although I had camped by myself in the bush before, this was my first droving trip alone.

That first night I camped beside a muddy water-hole in an outside channel of the Warrego River. Before sundown, after much running and chasing about, I finally caught and hobbled all the horses to stop them from straying. One grey mare, a real rogue, was hard to catch. Then, unpacking my food and swag, I soon had a fire going, chops grilling on the coals, and strong tea, well sugared, in my blackened, battered quart pot. (As well as a swag, every stockman and drover carried his own quart pot and a saddlebag to carry his cut lunches.)

As the sun set that evening and I watched its reddish glow fade into the darkness, the sound of clinking hobble chains and the donging horse bell was somehow reassuring. Without lantern or torch I rolled out my swag, wondering what my mates were doing in town, hoping there would be a couple of good cowboy pictures showing when I arrived in Bourke on Saturday.

I planned to visit the Greek cafe across the street from the pictures. That cafe not only sold the greatest ice-cream, it had this jukebox which could play your favourite record over and over, sometimes to the disgust of patrons having a meal. I knew about the picture house and the Greek cafe because this was not my first visit to Bourke. I had been there a short time before with Scobie, the great jockey, travelling in a truck carrying racehorses.

How well I remembered that first visit to New South Wales. Down there, everything seemed worse than it was at Cunnamulla for Aborigines. If they wanted to be served in hotels, they had to show "dog-tags". In Queensland at that time, some pubs would serve Murries, while others barred our people purely for being born Aboriginal.

Although I did not drink at that time (being under-age), when I did start later on I found it insulting to be asked for an exemption paper in New South Wales. I would tell the publican that I had no need of a "dog-tag" as I had no intention of becoming an honorary white man, which this little piece of paper was supposed to make me.

Even then I was learning about the power of words and how to use them against oppression and injustice. On entering a pub, mostly I would be told: "We don't serve you black bastards in here." I recall one day informing a large, red-faced publican that he reminded me of his outside shithouse, ugly to look at and stinking inside, so I was grateful that he wouldn't serve me. Besides which, I told him, it was much better to be a black bastard than a clapped-out white bastard.

Now, alone with that mob of horses, here I was heading back to Bourke again.

Throughout my droving life, I read the story of the past as it was told by the land. This night, I was camped on what had been until recently Tinnenburra station, a vast pastoral empire that had been resumed for soldier settlement and divided into many smaller stations.

Tinnenburra was once owned by a man called James Tyson — "Hungry Tyson" he was called in his heyday. Tinnenburra could boast of having the biggest shearing shed in the world, with 101 shearing stands in use at one time. An army of shed hands and stockmen were employed to muster the thousands of sheep shorn there.

The shearers' cooks kept busy feeding such a large crew — no refrigerators or fast food in them days. I had heard that instead of the usual big cast-iron cooking pots, on Tinnenburra the stewpot was like a huge steel tank, and it took four cooks to make enough stew to feed the horde of hungry men. As the stew slowly simmered, it was stirred by three of them cooks using oars from a rowing boat. A man was employed full-time to keep the fire going under this great stewpot.

But there was evidence of other histories long before Tyson's day. Chipped rocks and flints scattered around told of another age of the Kunja people, who still live in the area and can trace their ancestry back for thousands of generations. Many are the stories told of Tyson who was said to have had a good relationship with the local Aboriginal people, and for years many of them made their homes on Tinnenburra. But he was a hard man.

One night, sitting at a campfire talking to his stockmen, Tyson watched as one man rolled a cigarette, then struck a match to light his smoke. Tyson snorted in distaste. "You're sacked," he informed that stockman. "Why?" the stockman asked. "Because you're too wasteful, my good man. Striking a match while sitting beside a fire is a waste of matches — you could have lit your cigarette from the fire." Maybe this is where the saying "save a match and buy a sheep station" came from. Though it would take trillions of matches to buy such a vast empire as Tinnenburra.

One evening as darkness fell and the sounds of the night world took over, I fell to wondering what was fact and what was fiction or just bhulan-bhulan — an Aboriginal word which doesn't actually mean you're a bloody liar but is non-confrontational, as if to say: "it could be the truth if it's not made up."

At that time I had a limited knowledge of the ancient Aboriginal spirits and how they sent messages to mankind. I did know that they were not borne on the wings of alien doves or angels. The spirit messengers were animals, fish, all creatures of the earth, as well as the four winds ... a message might even be sent through the call of a bird. I had gathered such knowledge listening to Dreamtime stories of creation told at night in the Yumba.

At school, in the daytime, I was told other, Christian stories, and as a result some confusion crept into my mind. At school I learned about a heavenly Father, the unseen ruler of a kingdom in the sky, and I was also told about

Satan, the prince of darkness … At home I learned about
Mother Earth, a comforting reality, and was told about evil
spirits such as the Wham-Boo.

In time, I began to suspect there were neither good nor
evil spirits, only good and bad people who created them. I
stopped fearing the dead, ghosts and haunting spirits,
remaining wary only of the living. Yet I was aware of a
spirituality that came from within myself as well as from
nature and Mother Earth, which gave me strength.

Dreamtime

Out of the darkness of night
he came
carrying boomerang, waddy and spear:
a tribal man from the Dreamtime past.
Out of my swag I rose
staring in awe at this tribal man
bathed in a halo of light.

Waving his boomerang
he asked me questions,
speaking a lingo I understood.
"What have you done to my land?
Where does the meat of my tribe
roam now?
What of my berry roots and seeds?
What are these horses, cattle and sheep,
surveyors' pegs, boundary fences,
graded tracks upon my land?
They mean nothing to me.

"Twenty thousand years ago
my father in his wisdom
surveyed and mapped this land.
Markers of our kingdom
remain defined today —
unlike those boundary pegs
rotted and fallen by the way."

He threw his boomerang
in a curving arc:
it glittered and glowed
with shimmering light ...
Before my eyes the landscape changed:
vanished the fence and road,
gone the whiteman's meat,
cattle and sheep ...
even the man-made drought had gone
as the boomerang returned to his hand.

I gazed in awe
at waving grass
shrubs, berries, nuts and seeds:
those tribal meats
from Dreamtime past,
in my time grazed from existence.

"Where are they now,
my fruits, berries, nuts and seeds,
my medicine plants?
All of them gone,
disappeared from earth's face,
trampled and crushed
by the hard cloven hooves
of the whiteman's meat."

Still in a trance
I watched that old man
from the Dreamtime
grip his waddy and swing it around:
it was as though
in every colour of the rainbow,
in laser lights, a video clip appeared.
He showed me his world,
how he had left it,
then gave me a message,
the reason for his return.
I remember the words he spoke,
I remember them well.

"Look after this land
of your birth,

for the earth is mother
and father of all living things.
You live in heaven:
paradise is the earth,
and back to the earth
is where you will go.
Ours was a culture of sharing
and caring for land.
Not a culture of greed
and the raping of land.

"Let there be land for Dreamtime,
land for progress,
land set aside for the sake
of the animal world.
Land to be shared
by progress and Dreamtime both —
for a sharing of culture and land
is wiser than no land, no culture remaining.

"But always remember —
look after the land.
For earth is the mother,
life-blood of all our hopes.
My Dreamtime past you cannot change,
but the shaping of the future
and the protection of this land
you, with many others,
hold in your hands."

Then thrusting his spear into the ground
in a flash of light
back to the Deamtime past
went this tribal man.

Next day, by a boundary fence
stuck in the ground
I found a spear.
Now it stands in one corner
of my room.
It reminds me of that Dreamtime man,
whose words I remember so well.

"What have you done to my land?
The spirits of the earth —
can't you hear them crying
as the sacred soil
is raped and plundered?
What the rain does not wash away
the wind blows aside as dust.

"My Dreamtime past
you cannot change,
but the shaping of the future
and the protection of the land
you, and many others, hold in your hands.

"For earth is our Mother:
the past she holds
is hidden to many,
but everyone's future
lies in her being."

The spiritual feeling of my people was reinforced one night, while camped alone in the bush miles from any station homestead or town, with only a few horses for company. Lying in my swag, gazing upward, the starry sky was like some vast, glittering storybook made up of symbols, shapes and signs, a huge jigsaw puzzle scattered from horizon to horizon.

Venus, the evening star, like some precious opal, turned from a reddish glow to green and then acquired a magical whitish sparkle as it sank out of sight. There was also Orion, the saucepan, and lower down the Southern Cross shone like a beacon to lost travellers. The Milky Way and Magellan's Clouds lay scattered across the sky, a complete book in itself with many small clusters of glittering stars and the darker, clearly defined shape of the Emu.

In Dreamtime legend those star clusters are said to be eggs laid by this brilliantly coloured emu that strutted its path across the sky; the Milky Way, as it is called, is believed to be the dreaming track it left behind.

That great void up there was created when the Emu grew so obsessed with its own beauty that it decided to come down to earth to show off its grandeur. It landed on earth where it strutted about admiring its own appearance, fancying itself the brightest bird of all and causing much resentment as it flew around. So the Earth Spirit decided to punish the Emu, and chopped off its elegant, sparkling wings. Earthbound, the Emu was doomed to race across the ground like some aeroplane forever trying to take off to the heavens. Its colours faded to a drab, brownish grey as a warning never to put beauty before all else.

Now the flightless Emu lays its eggs upon the ground, while up above, in that dark empty space in the Milky Way, you can see the shape it left behind, with its unhatched cluster of eggs glittering in the Magellan Clouds.

That was just one story I pieced together that night from the big jigsaw in the sky as I pondered the riddle of the universe ...

Suddenly I was distracted by the almost human sound of a Curlew's scream ... or was it a Curlew? I sat up in my swag and looked around. What if this was a haunted place? Perhaps someone had been murdered under that mulga tree over there ... As I glanced around, the tree became a dark, swaying shape bending to the soft moan of the wind. Or maybe some alien encounter would take place ... what if one of them UFOs landed out on the grassy flat where the horses, themselves once alien to Australia, were now resting?

If you have ever argued with yourself, trying to dispel fear of the unknown when you are all alone, then you will understand how I felt that night. It is an argument I have had many times, and it has supported my conclusion that good and evil spirits come from within ourselves.

If some ghostly apparition did appear, I frantically wished it might be friendly and help me catch that mongrel grey mare at daybreak. As for the UFO, them aliens when they landed would be so superior that it would be pointless running away. Besides, I could learn a lot from an encounter like that. So, with the branches being twisted into imaginary shapes above, I pulled the blankets over my head and would have slept soundly but for another worrying thought ... What if some living maniac should chance upon my camp?

I began to recall gruesome murders in the outback I had heard of. Not far from here, a man had killed his mate with an axe, then burnt the body on a huge bonfire. Days after the murder, when the coals and ashes had finally cooled, the murderer, thinking he could never be caught because he would leave no evidence, sifted the ashes for fragments of bone and shovelled them down the deep, dry bore hole he and his mate had drilled. Much later, police investigating his mate's disappearance recovered those fragments from the bottom of what became known as Murder Bore, and the murderer was convicted.

More gruesome tales came to mind as I sat up once again and stared nervously about. From the trees came the soft, contented cooing of roosting birds. Yet to my ears it seemed to have a more sinister meaning. Maybe there was someone or something behind that tree ... The dull, clinking sound of a hobble chain as a feeding horse moved a few steps to another fresh tuft of grass sounded more like someone creeping closer to my lonely camp ... One more peek around, then: "Bugger this, I got sixty kilometres to ride tomorrow, better get some sleep!" It was on such nights, alone, that I experienced strange dreams as I slept.

I have always been interested in science and the future as much as the Dreaming history. I admire astronauts greatly, yet I do not envy their achievements. Like them, I have looked on sights that most people only dream of, here on mother earth, which we all belong to.

I recall one wintry night after a long day in the saddle driving a small mob of horses to a station then returning late to a drovers' camp. As I rode along a seldom used bush track, the sun began to sink and the bushland came alive with the bleating of sheep and lowing of cattle as they sought rest and safety in numbers from foxes and dingoes. Then, as darkness fell, the kangaroos and other night-foraging creatures came out to feed while from the trees came the soft sound of roosting birds.

Soon a full moon cast a silvery sheen across that land-scape of sandhills. A cold breeze sang through the belah trees, distorting bushes and branches into weird shapes. Suddenly the sounds of the night, the shadows and swaying branches seemed somehow menacing.

I was about to urge my horse into a trot when I heard this loud snarling that turned into a high-pitched, blood-curdling scream, the like of which I had never heard before. My horse stopped with ears pricked, staring into the shifting shadows. A cold shiver that had nothing to do with the south wind went through my body as I peered around, talking softly to my horse to reassure him, patting his neck.

What animal or alien creature had made that unnatural sound? I was torn between the urge to make a headlong gallop for camp and the desire to find out. Was this some evil spirit at work, maybe a fight between the Christian devil and the Dreamtime Dibble-Dibble? Oh, how I wished I had not stopped to inspect a couple of birds' nests on my way home, or to watch that rabbit run up a hollow log! I could have been back at camp long before sundown.

But soon this fear of the unknown was replaced by something stronger: that insatiable curiousity of mine. Urging my horse off the track we both peered intently ahead, reading many shapes into the wind-blown trees and shadows.

Meanwhile, those murderous screams had started up again, and my horse began to whinny. It stopped suddenly: and then I saw this huge, dark screaming creature shaped like a ball come tumbling fast in and out of the dense shadows behind the bushes and around the tree trunks. Out into the silvery, moonlit clearing rolled the creature, still screaming its devilish delight, tumbling backwards and forwards.

More fascinated than frightened, I urged my horse closer. At this point the creature stopped rolling and screaming, and as I watched in disbelief, you could say it parted in two! Sitting open-mouthed, I stared at the biggest fox and the largest feral cat I have ever seen.

The next moment they began to fight again. Their battle cries would have carried for miles. At last the fox broke away, whimpering and making subdued yapping sounds, defeated in combat by the cat.

Gee, I thought, imagination can create many fearful things. Yet I felt a strange contentment in my heart as I headed towards camp, for I reminded myself that I had indeed seen two creatures alien to my dreaming. And believe me, foxes can make more ungodly sounds than their muted barks.

I felt refreshed after being the one human being to have had a ringside seat for that battle in the bush, and grateful that the full moon had enabled me to see such a spectacular sight … A sight that no astronaut would ever see on his journey to that same moon, our beaming friend that has already become a dreaming track for future generations.

Yet again I was aware of how privileged we are to be a living part of mother earth — and perhaps there are more mysteries buried in the earth than on the moon.

One day I would love to be able to visit the moon, yet without the aid of a space suit. I would like to light a campfire there, boil my billy and sleep in my swag. How wondrous that would be, staring down at mother earth the way I used to lie in my swag gazing upward at the glowing sky.

Soon after that lone trip with the horses, I was off on another droving job. I recall George, one of the local drover bosses, saying: "Come work with me, boy. Town no good for you." So I became one of the Aboriginal crew of three that George hired to drove about five hundred head of cattle south across the Queensland border … Once again, I found myself headed for Bourke.

Both the other members of that crew were older and more experienced than me. Bulla was in charge. He was an old man, born into tribal life on a distant cattle station. He could neither read nor write but he was a great stockman. Tommy was in his twenties, also a good stockman, but he lacked Bulla's wisdom. And of course there was me, the great adventurer.

What a journey that turned out to be! Before starting out with the cattle we gathered the horses. George pointed to a pretty piebald mare. "Her name is Picture, she's just broken in," he told me. "She'll buck a bit but I want you to quieten her down. If she's quiet by the time you return, I'll give you a bonus."

Right there, on the edge of town near the railway line, Bulla, George and Tommy helped mount me up on Picture. In a flash the little mare was away, bolting and bucking across the open ground, across the railway line, her front legs still hobbled. "Oh by gee, she's gonna fall," I thought. Cursing under my breath, I somehow managed to get Picture under control and back to the waiting men, mindful of George shouting: "Don't hurt her, boy, don't upset her, she belongs to the wife!"

Meanwhile, the wife was being more vocal than her husband in offering advice. "Picture's such a lovely horse," she said as I dismounted. Well, in spite of the fact that I could have been badly hurt, even killed, as Picture bolted and bucked across that railway line, I had to agree — she was a lovely horse (only to look at).

We headed off with a packhorse plant of twenty horses. The packhorses carried our food and swags. There had been heavy rains a few weeks before and the Warrego was in flood. Releasing the cattle that had arrived by train from the trucking yards, we headed south. A few kilometres out of town we discovered the river was rising fast. An outside channel of the river about three feet deep was a raging torrent.

George came down to us in his car. "Swim them across," he said. So we did. The cattle waded over, then the horses were herded across. Bulla and Tommy urged their horses into the stream, until at last only me and a very water-shy Picture remained. She would not enter the water no matter how hard I urged her, even with George shouting advice all the time. At last I drove my spurs into her girth. Facing the water, she gave an almighty buck in the air, spinning to the right. I was thrown flat-out in a huge belly flop, landing in the muddy, raging floodwater as Picture galloped across to join the other horses.

Suddenly I realised that my precious Akubra hat was being washed downstream. Regardless of Munta-guttas or whatever else the floodwaters concealed, I swam after that hat, the first new one I had ever bought, the first I'd ever worn that fitted my head. Meanwhile, George, resting on the car bonnet, was shouting: "Ya frightened the mare, boy, ya made her buck. Look after her properly, I'm telling ya, she belongs to the wife!"

Wringing wet, hat restored to my head, I ended up wading across the flooded creek to take up my ongoing battle with Picture, who had been recaptured by Bulla. In this strange, undignified way I crossed my first real flooded creek as a drover.

The low flooded country along the Warrego was not strange to me, with its many large red sandhills (like the one where we used to play as kids) stretching to the New South Wales border. Soon we had to cross the flooded channel again, but here it was much deeper.

The cattle were swum over, but we could not cross with our laden packhorses. So Bulla decided we should camp on one of those big sandhills that first night. The weather was fine and there was no floodwater outside the channel. Tomorrow, Bulla said confidently, the waters would be low enough for the packhorses to cross.

Alas, next morning the floodwaters had risen and broken the banks of the Warrego and the outside channel. There was water everywhere. The only dry piece of land was that big sandhill where we were camped.

By nightfall it was raining again. So there we were, the three of us, camped under a small tarpaulin, the horses eating the sparse grass growing amid the hopbush. We were stranded. The cattle were long gone up ahead and safely grazing on high ground.

We sat on that big sandhill for ten days. In this time we had eaten the few tins of meat we had with us. Luckily there were a few rabbits on the hill, and as the evening shadows lengthened we would sit there while Bulla fashioned throwing-sticks with his pocket knife. With these we soon knocked off all those rabbits on that hill. A sand goanna which had sought refuge there ended up as supper one night, and so did a couple of kangaroos and a porcupine. We had plenty of flour, tea and sugar, but after ten days the water level was still not falling, and Bulla decided we would return to town, a ride of some ten or twelve kilometres.

It would have been too hard to ride upstream all the way — the horses would soon have tired. So we headed off east to the built-up highway, some eight kilometres away, sloshing through knee-deep water with one short cross-channel swim. Not a single piece of dry land did we see until we reached that highway.

That evening, back in Cunnamulla, we ate a hearty meal at the cafe, and when the floodwaters finally receded we resumed our journey to Bourke and back, which proved a relatively uneventful experience after such an adventurous beginning.

While we'd been stranded on the hill, Bulla had got me to ride Picture every day. I spent a lot of time with her, even riding her bareback, knowing I was in control on the soft, heavy sand. She was a quiet but somewhat dejected horse by the time we returned to town. I pointed this out to George, recalling our conversation before we had started out. But somehow he found other topics to talk about. Needless to say, I never got that two pounds bonus.

Both us and the horses were saved by that sandhill. That loose red sand had been heaped up over hundreds of thousands of years and had saved many, many animals from drowning.

Sadly, when I now walk on what remains of the sandhill back home at Cunnamulla, I wonder at the devastation I see. These days the sand is removed to build levee banks against floodwater, which seems a short-sighted policy to me.

One day, I believe, the floodwater will cover the levee banks, and there will be no big red sandhill remaining as a natural refuge. For humans and animals alike, the only escape route will be by air or boat. Perhaps the power of nature and the mythology of the Munta-gutta will have the last say when the sandhill around the site of the Yumba finally disappears.

The New South Wales town of Bourke held another memory for me. Dad's death was the first time in my life I shed real tears of grief. I was in my early teens when he died, during the first of many Christmases I spent away from home.

I had been working around Bourke and was having a well-earned rest, the boss drover paying for me to stay at a boarding house and look after his horses, grazing close by. One morning a policeman came up to the boarding house and told me that Dad had died of a heart attack. The news brought a deadening of the spirit — the same feeling that I felt a few years later when Mum died. It was a new emotional experience for me. A sense of deep, irreplaceable loss.

There was no more droving work on offer at the time, and I was stony broke. The lady who owned the boarding house was comforting, and we discussed how I could get back to Cunnamulla in time for Dad's funeral. There were no buses; I could try to hitch a ride, but in them days it was a journey of 240 kilometres along dusty, corrugated dirt roads.

Learning of my predicament, a man who worked on a nearby station said: "I might be able to help you, mate. I'll get you a ticket on the mail plane that leaves here tomorrow if you promise to come back in the New Year and do some work for me." I had never met this man before, yet he was willing to trust me to come back to work off that airfare. He was truly compassionate.

Next day I caught that mail plane from Bourke to Cunnamulla. It was my first plane ride, yet I remember little of the flight. I knew that the small old double-wing Royal Mail plane which I had almost shot out of the sky a few years before was now replaced by a much larger DC3 aircraft.

And I recall that as we approached Cunnamulla we flew wide to the east of the Yumba airspace. Even so, I could plainly see the scattered shacks, tents and humpies which seemed to be fenced in on three sides, by the red sandhill and green hopbush to the east, the white-painted cemetery fence to the north, and the tree-lined riverbanks to the west.

As I looked down my sense of loss was combined with a comforting contentment that I was returning home — not so much to Cunnamulla, but to the Yumba and my people, who all shared my family's great loss.

Funerals have always held great significance for Aboriginal people: they are the only occasions that bring many people together, not only in grieving but in remembrance of happier if harder times.

After we had buried Dad, I caught the mail truck into New South Wales again to work for a while quietening some Shetland ponies for that kind man who had paid my airfare.

Alas, I cannot recall his name, but it has always been

people like him and my parents who have given me faith and hope in life. Faith, not in mystical gods, but in living people shaping a better future for everyone. Nothing ever happens on its own: we have to help it along.

My next droving trip was with my mates Bunji and Gundi. Bunji (the amateur jockey I mentioned earlier) was a few years older than me and Gundi, and had recently got married. Bunji's father was a boss drover, and because he was busy with other mobs at the time, he hired Bunji as boss, plus me and Gundi, to collect six hundred head of cattle from an outback station. We were to bring them down to another station near Cunnamulla. The trip would take us about a week.

The cattle had been walked from the Northern Territory, together with another six hundred head, on a droving trip that had lasted over three months. The drover who had brought them from the far north was supposed to leave half the mob at one station (which he had done) and then bring on the rest to the second station. But after such a long time on the road he was anxious to head back home with his tired horses and men.

Well, after a night of talking with that dusty, bearded drover, Bunji, Gundi and me headed off with them six hundred head of cattle. After three months on the track them cattle were so well broken in that one man or boy could handle them alone. I remember that our rations and swags were carried in a small, rubber-tyred milk van, a sulky, used during my schooldays to carry a couple of milk and cream cans stowed under the high driver's seat. Pulling this sulky was a slab-sided, black, cantankerous, one-eyed horse called Charlie, well known as a bolter.

Reaching our first camp, Gundi, who never cooked before was appointed as cook. He decided to make a damper from the bag of plain flour we had with us. My mate John the cook had told me that "ya gotta have baking powder to make damper", but there was none amongst the meagre rations in the milk cart. "Can't I make it without baking powder?" Gundi asked. Well, for the rest of the week we lived on the worst, soggiest dampers I have ever tasted.

Gundi was always testing things out. He had grand ideas of making millions owning stations or finding gold or opal mines. It's not that Gundi was an outrageous liar, just that he had these great imaginative powers he used to explain away his failings.

Like on one occasion after we'd left school he claimed (while we were mustering cattle and he became separated) to have chased on horseback a fair dinkum Tasmanian tiger in outback Queensland.

Another time, Gundi went missing while mustering stock in a paddock of maybe a hundred thousand acres covered in stony hills and thick scrub. After returning on time for the evening meal, as usual, he dismounted from his horse and began his spiel.

"Ya not gonna believe this, mate, but I was attacked by this kangaroo, you know, behind the red hill up by Gidyea Creek, over that way," he said, waving his arm in a westerly direction.

"I had this big mob of wild cleanskin cattle under control, all on my own, heading for the dam to meet up with you fellas, when I pulls up for a drink of water from that native well. You know, where ya head into that gorge.

"Well after I finished drinking, this great big red kangaroo about seven foot tall comes hopping out of the Mulga and heads straight for me. So I stands up to scare that roo away.

"But true mate, he just keeps coming towards me, so I starts yelling then swearing, waving my hat around, but this bloody great roo keeps coming, then starts attacking me without warning. Just comes hopping up and lets fly with a Kung Fu kick to the gut.

"So I got mad at that big red roo: I take side steps when he comes in to attack again, grab his tail and flip him over onto his back and give him a good thrashing with my belt then turn him loose. True as God, mate, maybe that roo thought I was drinking at his private waterhole."

Needless to say, we could never fathom if Gundi had become lost or just lay down and dozed off to sleep under some shady tree, only dreaming of such things.

Back on track, the world seemed a brighter place after we delivered those cattle, some twenty kilometres from Cunnamulla, then headed off for town with Bunji driving the sulky and Gundi and me riding behind, driving the loose horses.

We were eager to get home. It was Saturday — cowboy picture night. But Bunji, trying to set an example as the boss, kept on driving steadily and slowly. Too slowly, Gundi and me thought as the shadows lengthened and the sun dipped into the western sky.

"We gonna be late for the picture, mate," Gundi said as he rode along, voicing my own fears. "At this pace it'll be sundown before we get home. We gotta get that bloody milk cart going faster."

"Maybe Charlie could take fright and bolt," I suggested.

"Okay," said Gundi, "let's give it a try." So he trotted up alongside the milk cart and began to talk loudly to Bunji, waving his hat in the air at the same time.

One-eyed Charlie heard this loud voice, and saw the hat being waved in a menacing fashion above his blinkers. He gave one loud snort then took off flat-out down the dirt track towards home. Bunji's piercing screams — "Ya made the bloody horse bolt! Ya made him bolt!" only convinced Charlie that something or someone was after him, and he ran even faster.

"C'mon! We gotta keep up!" Gundi shouted with a gleeful whoop. Laughing and joking, we sent them loose horses galloping after the milk cart, while Bunji, perched high on his seat, did his best to check Charlie's speed. "Keep back!" he yelled, "you'll frighten Charlie all over again!" After a few kilometres everything was again under control and for a while we rode along quite steadily, with Bunji holding Charlie to a snail's pace.

Then Gundi said: "He's going too slow, mate, it's your turn. Get Charlie going again! Them pictures will be over before we get there."

So I trotted up to Bunji, praising him for the feat he had just performed in bringing Charlie under control. "Gee, he was travelling fast, mate," I shouted at the top of my voice. "Lucky the milk cart didn't capsize when ya came around that sharp bend, ya know the wheel only just missed that tree stump — that was great driving, mate!"

"Keep back!" shrieked Bunji as I drew nearer. "If you fellas ride up here again I'll sack ya!"

"What's that, mate?" I yelled, trotting closer and waving my hat.

More snorts, then one-eyed Charlie was off again, with Bunji screaming, "Ya made the horse bolt! Ya sacked! Ya both sacked!" and waving his arms, making Charlie run even faster.

"What about our pay! Come back here and give us our pay!" shrieked Gundi, doubled over laughing in sheer delight.

"Ya sacked! Sacked, both of ya!" we heard Bunji call back.

We laughed as we galloped closer to town, drooling over

the thought of ice-cream and a cowboy picture. We got to
the pictures with an hour to spare. By then Bunji had
forgiven us. Perhaps he was secretly anxious to get back as
soon as possible to see the new picture on in town.

In the darkened picture show, me and Gundi were happy
just sitting alongside certain girls we liked, feeding them
Columbines or Minties. But we were growing up, and it was
about this time back in the Yumba I would be occasionally
talking to some older men, uncles and such, when a teenage girl might come walking between the camps. Quite
often them old men would say, "Don't go looking at that
one, boy, she's wrong yhudie for you." In this way, they
warned us of the complexities of Aboriginal marriage laws
which at one time were observed by every language group.

Yet I was still at the stage where all I wanted to do was
double a certain black-haired beauty on that Malvern Star
bicycle of my dreams. She was from the Yumba; as neighbours, we grew up together. I didn't even want to hold her
hand.

Soon after, that notion of owning a shining bike was to
become a discarded dream, replaced by visions of me riding
off into the sunset (or sunrise) on a prancing, blood-red
chestnut stallion, with that same girl perched on the saddle
pommel. Then I began to wonder what would happen if
that horse went lame. I would have to discard the beautiful
girl … for I was now in love with Prince, the imaginary
chestnut stallion, and my desire was to see what lay beyond
not just the next hill but the one after that, to venture
through other flooded landscapes, as well as dry creeks and
rivers …

9
MY LITERARY LIFE

STRANGE, YOU KNOW, after each adventure I would always say, "I'm gonna write a story about that!" To which my mates would always reply, "Yer, yer, mate, one day …" Well, for the next forty years all I wrote were a few letters. The fourth letter was to a mate of mine. I did not post that letter, but instead turned it into a poem … After that, I wrote maybe one hundred poems and have had four books published, with another three or four underway. I write to create awareness of different experiences, to record history seldom taught, and most of all to entertain. Now writing, not riding, is my career.

For me the power of words and the transcendence of imagination, from drawing forbidden images in the dust of the Yumba to the wonders of television and the word processor, is magical. Humour is especially important, even in serious writing — without it I could not write at all.

I have described how I live now in Cunnamulla on the very spot where the biggest and best oranges in the world once grew, in an orchard guarded from invasion by a cockatoo chained to a gum tree. All my writing has been done here. And I have told how the screeching of wild cockatoos often shatters my concentration so that I often go outside to curse them birds invading the silence of my literary orchard, from which I reap another kind of harvest.

Indoors, some strange things have been known to happen. Largely because of my inexperience with the computer and the importance of filing and saving stories and poems. I once had to rewrite a 3000-word story four times because I had forgotten to save it. When that happened, I screeched and cursed louder than all them cockatoos, even inventing new swear words. But the next time it happened, I just walked away in silence.

For a long time afterwards, I had pasted around the screen of my word processor these large signs: SAVE! YA SILLY BUGGER, SAVE! These inventions certainly are magical: many times I have seen thousands of words disappear for ever by the mere touch of a single key.

The cockatoos always seem to distract me when I have deadlines to meet for articles and books. I blame them birds, yet I am also capable of conjuring up for myself a thousand reasons why I should not write, when it is painfully obvious I have to get stuck into it. Like certain school students when they have homework they should be doing, or when their parents ask them to do something for them and they reply: "Yer, yer, in a minute." I believe this reluctance applies to everyone when they are faced with something they know they should be doing.

Before I got my word processor I used a typewriter, and one night I had a deadline to meet for a story. I looked with something like loathing at that typewriter in the corner of my room and then a brilliant idea came to me: why not just place a piece of paper in the machine, turn off the lights and go to sleep … in the morning that blank page would surely be filled with the best story ever written, composed by magic guardian creatures that would come while I was sleeping. So, switching off the lights I tumbled into bed smiling instead of worrying about that deadline.

After a sound, refreshing sleep I rose early next morning and, still smiling, peeked around the door at my typewriter. I was half-expecting that some sort of miracle would have happened: alas, only the same blank page greeted me. "That's strange," I thought. "I was sure those little magical beings would help me out in my hour of need."

Thankfully, out of this make-believe exercise came a greater understanding of reality. It dawned on me that the only way a page was ever gonna get filled was by me, who had the *creative*, not magical, power to make things happen. Sitting at my typewriter I finally got down to work and filled that blank page plus another twenty, with the realisation that writing only becomes a reality when your thoughts are translated into words, and you've had a good sleep.

When people ask me questions at literary functions, or when I talk to schoolchildren, I have to come up with answers on any subject. Little children especially often ask real awkward questions. At one Queensland preschool, I was introduced to a group of little kids who sat cross-legged on the floor with eager anticipation on their faces.

"Now Herb is an author," their teacher informed them. "Can anyone tell me what an author is?"

Well, this little boy about four years old jumped up and blurted out: "An — an author is — is a per-sun, with no mummy and no daddy!"

After the laughter died down the teacher suggested the children would love to hear a Dreamtime story. So I told them how the Pelican was created …

"There was this lazy man who would always become sick

or get a sore leg whenever it was time for the warriors of his tribe to go hunting. Then, after they had left the camp, he would raid the tribe's fish-traps and eat all the fish, breaking the tribal law that everyone should make their contribution.

"As time went by he became fatter and lazier than ever, and the hunters wondered why there were never any fish in their traps.

"One day they decided to spy on Big Mouth, as he was known, and they caught him stealing the fish. Justice was swift: he was clubbed on the head with nulla-nullas, then thrown across a partly submerged log near the water's edge. His arms and legs were broken, and he was left to die, pleading to the spirits for mercy with his last breath.

"Well, the spirits decided to save him, not out of pity or because he had been so harshly dealt with by tribal law, but as a warning to all future law-breakers of what would happen to them if they were caught. Yet they could not save him in the form of a man. So this is what they did —"

At this point the children, enthralled, sat silently waiting for me to continue.

"Those spirits told that man: 'Seeing that as a human you were too lazy to walk about and hunt kangaroo and emu, we will give you short legs, finishing where they are broken off at your knees. And because your mouth was used for lying and eating all the tribe's fish, you and your kind will eat nothing else but fish for ever.' — And that is how the Pelican got its bill, which it uses as a fish-trap. For the Pelican cannot walk away from the riverbank and eat fruits and seeds like other birds ... fruits and seeds which that tribesman was too lazy to harvest when he was a human being.

"Then the spirits went on: 'Your broken arms will become short wings, so that you can fly from one waterhole to another.' " I ended the story by saying: "Today, whenever you see a pelican, remember that it was created as a warning against laziness and greed, and taking what is not yours."

I then asked the children if they had any questions. The same little boy who had given his definition of an author raised his hand. "Hey," he said, "that was only one pelican them spirits made. Where did all the others come from? You've got to have two to breed more of them." (I learned later that his father was a farmer, and he knew about sheep and cattle breeding.)

Well, I scratched my head, wondering at his reasoning. He had come up with a real tricky question all right. Then I recalled how this story was also told about a woman. "Well," I said slowly, "it just so happened that at another waterhole further west there lived this other tribe, and lo and behold, a woman of that tribe was also getting sick every time the other women went to gather yams or fruits, and she too stole fish from the nets when they were away from the camp.

"So she suffered the same fate as the man and the spirits changed *her* into a pelican. Then both them pelicans flew west and met up at this big waterhole, might be Lake Eyre, and started breeding.

"And that's why, after a big flood in the inland of Australia, thousands and thousands of pelicans migrate there to breed and nest, many only to die when the floodwater dries up and turns to salt."

Sometimes I point out to schoolkids that before Captain Cook arrived in Australia, there were hundreds of different Australian Aboriginal languages. I tell them that when I was a boy, many people in the Yumba could express themselves clearly in their tribal language, but sometimes had trouble speaking fluent English. To them, English was a foreign language. This did not mean there was any lack of intelligence on their part; after all, even cockatoos and galahs can learn to speak English quite well … yet I have never heard one of them birds speak an Aboriginal Australian language.

I recall how one day, when us kids made our way to school along the riverbank, we came across a family that'd been removed from the station that had been their ancestral home since the Dreamtime. Now, displaced from their tribal territory, they were camped in a tent.

They had a boy our age called Pidgeon, and we became mates. Unlike us Murries who had lived in the Yumba all our lives, this boy had a better understanding of his own language than English. His parents, who had never seen a town before, let alone a school, decided Pidgeon should have some English learning, so he began to go off to school with us. He had a rusty old pushbike.

One morning, walking past his family's tent, we asked if Pidgeon was coming to school with us that day. Then this old lady, standing tall and straight, barefooted before an open fire, yelled out to Pidgeon in her own language; it was easy to tell she was scolding him. She turned to us and said: "Nar, that boy he can't go school, he sick today, that Pidgeon."

Meanwhile Pidgeon had appeared in the tent entrance, looking as healthy as usual. The old lady spoke to him again: "If ya too sick to go ta school, ya jump on that pushbike and go 'n tell that Ambulance man to come down and pick ya up straight away."

Puzzled by this strange request, we headed off to school, and a few minutes later Pidgeon, riding his bike, caught us up and came with us.

Another day, that same old lady gave Pidgeon a warning as we headed for the river. We had asked whether Pidgeon could come swimming with us. "Nar, nar," she said, "water too deep. Munta-gutta over there in them caves." After much pleading by Pidgeon she relented, saying: "Okay, okay, boy. You go swimming with them boys. But remember, if ya go in deep water and get drowned, don't bother coming home crying to me, 'cause I'll give ya a real good floggin'."

Some years later, at a small hotel in Queensland near the New South Wales border, another incident demonstrated the power of words to me. I was returning home from a droving trip. By this time I was old enough to enter hotels … but, as it turned out, not old enough — or white enough — to get a drink.

I was hitching a ride back home with two other drovers from Cunnamulla, both white. We pulled up to this wayside pub and walked inside. The human Germ behind the bar asked: "What d'you want?" My mate and his son both said: "Three beers, please." To which the Germ answered: "I can serve you two, but I can't serve *him*" — pointing at me.

At this, old Charlie sounded off, cursing worse than me. For the first and only time he praised my virtues, saying that if I was good enough to work with, I was good enough to drink with. By now the Germ was standing well back behind the bar, trying to intimidate us by fondling a baseball bat. He ended up by calling in his mate, the gungi bal. I did not get my beer and my two withew friends refused their drinks, but they continued with the heated debate.

Eventually we left, with the Germ and the gungi bal standing in the doorway of that isolated hotel and us still hurling insults. I recall my mate informing them both in a loud voice as he got into his car: "I don't know where they breed vermin like you, but I feel sure there musta been some horrible mistake when you were born."

This to me was more intoxicating than alcohol. Words, the sheer power of them, could be as cutting as a dozen double-edged swords. I was unknowingly committing such incidents to memory. Years later, when I became a writer, they would be committed to paper.

I have already said that I choose to write about things I know best, my own experiences and surroundings, and the people I have known. Just looking out of my window or back door has had much to do with the telling of this story, with conjuring up memories.

From my writing desk I have an unobstructed view of the Catholic church and the convent school where I was refused entry years ago, in spite of the best efforts of my cousin Nell. It was a strange experience recently to spend an hour or so there at that school, talking about the importance of literature and learning.

My travels also bring me back to people. On a stopover at Kuala Lumpur airport in Malaysia, not long ago, I was warmly greeted by a lady who obviously knew me, yet I could not remember who she was. Then I realised she was one of the teaching nuns from that Catholic school in Cunnamulla, on holiday with her sister. You know, I had seldom seen that teaching sister walking around the almost deserted streets of our country town, yet I came across her there in Asia, amid teeming masses of people.

We chatted for a while; we had both arrived from London after being in Scotland, where she had visited the home of her ancestors and I gave a storytelling session at the Edinburgh Book Festival.

Another chance encounter happened on my first visit to Germany, in Berlin. I was giving a reading at the House of World Cultures, a short distance from the old Reichstag building. Lo and behold, giving a stage performance between those two historic buildings was my good mate Mandawuy Yunupingu, lead singer of Yothu Yindi. We had met often before, and I had seen and heard many of his performances on television and radio, and had visited him in Arnhem Land, in the Northern Territory.

Since that day in Berlin I have attended concerts he has given in Sydney and Melbourne, as well as Köln in Germany and Amsterdam in Holland. Our paths have even crossed at the airport in Bangkok.

Every memorable incident from my past or present life is important in creating stories. From the Yumba shack of my childhood and those dusty stock routes, where sometimes in stifling heat you would see mirages of a windmill or house suspended in the sky, as dancing willy-willys spiralled across the dry landscape like devils dancing their way to hell, to the many overseas places I have visited in the past handful of years.

All told, it has been a journey of enlightenment, and as I have journeyed I have been aware that it would all be meaningless without a sense of humour to keep everything in perspective along the way. Otherwise, how could I compare, say, shopping at Harrods in London to my shopping excursions in Charleville all those years ago, when that bloody great pet ram would always end up eating our bread, and us kids would go back empty-handed, cursing and crying.

Or, how could I compare a day at Royal Ascot with the

Birdsville outback races? One gentleman I met at Ascot did. Standing behind me waiting to be served at a bar, this fella wearing top hat and morning suit tapped me on the shoulder and, perhaps after eyeing my battered Akubra hat, remarked in a real cultured English voice: "By Joves, my good man, I do believe you get served faster at the Birdsville races than you do here." We then began to compare customs, how at the Birdsville races very few people bought a glass of beer, wine or whatever — they bought their beer by the carton and spirits by the bottle, then sat in the dust and drank their fill as the horses thundered around the dirt track, leaving behind them a large, hovering cloud of dust.

Last year, travelling by train at a speed of up to three hundred kilometres an hour from London to Paris in the English Channel tunnel, sitting in luxury with telephone and fax machines at hand, I recalled them old steam trains that rattled and swayed at about fifty kilometres an hour, and how the smoke and cinders flew back into your face when you stuck your head out of the window.

Yet they were more exciting in their way: for on the cross-Channel train there were no railway workers to wave at you from isolated verandas as them old steam trains chugged past, and the train did not have to give loud whistles to clear kangaroos, emus or herds of grazing sheep, cattle and horses from the tracks.

Travelling by train through the German countryside, I was always looking out for native animals like deer, wolves or bears, but mostly I glimpsed small herds of black-and-white dairy cattle near some farmhouse. What a contrast to the great, open grazing herds I knew in the outback!

Once I caught sight of a lone shepherd tending a few black sheep. It was like some scene from biblical times, this ancient, bearded shepherd walking with the aid of a long, crooked wooden pole near an isolated village. "That's the nearest thing to a German drover I'll ever see," I thought, my camera clicking furiously as the train sped past.

But a few days later, while being shown around Dresden in the early morning, within sight of the River Elbe, I came upon a German drovers' camp almost in the centre of that famous city. Inside a sheep yard bordered by plastic were about a thousand sheep, in full view of office blocks, historic castles, churches and the Opera House.

"Pull up, pull up!" I yelled to my host, "I gotta see this! A bloody mob of sheep back there in a sheep break! This I gotta inspect."

He turned around and we drove back and parked on the riverbank. I already had one snapshot of a German drover, but no one was tending them sheep in that plastic yard. "What are they doing there?" I asked my host, named Uwe (pronounced like You ... or like Ewe, as in sheep). "If these bloody drovers were in Australia and had their sheep still in the yard at this time of day they'd be sacked! Them sheep should be let out to feed."

Then Uwe informed me that in many parts of Germany, including Dresden, no one was allowed to erect buildings which would obstruct a view of the river frontage or hinder access to it. When summer came, the grass grew high and instead of using mowing machines that would add noise and pollution to the city, nearby farmers were allowed to graze their sheep along the riverbank. The farmer would leave his sheep there and come along each day to shift his flock a few yards ... unlike Australia, where you had to move a flock sometimes ten kilometres a day.

What a wonderful idea, I thought, recalling my first visit to Canberra, where I had stared in awe at the wide, shaded footpaths that lined most streets. Grass grew everywhere. At that time there was a big drought in outback Australia.

When someone asked me my impressions of our national

capital, I replied with enthusiasm: "What a town! It sure is a wonderful place. Why, drovers could feed a million head of starving stock around these streets. All that bloody good stock feed going to waste while animals starve in the bush! And that big waterhole in front of the station homestead — it could come in handy, too."

I had admired Lake Burley Griffin, with its spouting fountain, while the High Court building reminded me of a giant fodder silo, a little way from the main homestead — Parliament House.

I did convey my thoughts to a couple of politicians I met, with the further suggestion that perhaps they might consider moving the national capital to Cunnamulla. Then them hardworking drovers could ply their trade around them wide grassy streets of outback Canberra.

All my life I have searched for awareness and enlightenment by asking questions … questions which were not always answered. I was sometimes caned at school for asking questions (I realised later that most of the time I was questioning beliefs and attitudes that others seemed to take for granted), and around the campfire in the Yumba I would sometimes be given a clout across the ear for the same reason.

Travelling overseas helped me to think again about things I had once thought were true. For years after leaving school, then working mostly as a drover and stockman, and seeing a great deal of inland Australia yet little of the big cities or even the more settled rural areas, I assumed that "yumbas" existed only around outback towns, and were inhabited solely by Aboriginal people. So you can imagine my reaction when I realised that "yumbas" exist in different forms in almost every country of the world.

This realisation came to me on the other side of the world in Berlin, shortly after the Berlin Wall had come tumbling down and East and West Germany were (in theory) once more united. The comparison between the east and west was very clear: dilapidated buildings and poverty to the east, while to the west was evidence of a more lavish lifestyle and great wealth.

One evening I was being shown around a quiet eastern suburb, where many Turkish people had settled, when we came across this goat yard … only a few miles from the city centre. Imagine my delight! The yard was made from saplings and rabbit netting, exactly like others I had seen on many rundown Australian farms. Inside were five goats, plus a few chooks.

What a sight that was to please the heart of someone like me, who had just been thinking, "these poor fellas living here in this famous city, they got no front or back yards to play in". So that tumbledown goat yard in the midst of high-rise buildings and busy traffic, with people all around talking in German, Russian and Turkish, reminded me of home.

A few hundred yards further we crossed a narrow canal bridge that spanned part of the River Spree. This bridge had once been a military checkpoint between East and West Germany. Here, buildings were few and there was a sense of open space … yet all around huge building cranes blotted the skyline: never in my life had I seen so much construction going on in one city. Here in Berlin, there was surely as much building happening as in the whole of Australia.

I wandered over that bridge with Sally, my Australian friend and guide, who lived in Berlin. She showed me many out-of-the way places where none of the usual tourist guides would ever go.

Summer days are longer in Europe than in Australia; a dimming daylight lingers on until nine or ten at night, and it was already pretty late as we reached an open space across the bridge, once a no-man's land where many escapees had been shot trying to flee the eastern sector of the city. Here the road was narrow; a splintered, unpainted railing and rusty wire fence acted as a safety guard for cars, which might otherwise crash down the levee bank — about a thirty foot drop.

Resting on that fence and looking down, I saw this cluster of shacks and humpies made from bricks, tin, wood and torn, flapping tarpaulins, while other people were living in what looked like discarded car bodies. Coals and pieces of half-burnt board marked open fireplaces. "Wow!" was all I could exclaim, "a yumba in Berlin! A shantytown in no-man's land!"

I really felt for them people down there — yet they were not living under the same conditions of racial segregation, disadvantage and oppression that had been imposed on my people in Australia. They were experiencing a political segregation, not based on colour.

Sally pointed out one of these "yumba" dwellers as he emerged from his humpy and began speaking into a mobile phone. He was quite well-dressed. She told me that although many of these people were destitute, real refugees without housing or work, others lived here simply to avoid the increasing costs of accommodation.

This story began in the Yumba on the eastern bank of the Warrego River in outback Queensland, almost a lifetime ago. These final pages are being completed on the banks of the Seine, in the Australia Council studio at the Cité Internationale des Arts in the heart of Paris, camping just across the creek from Notre Dame.

This is a huge arts complex, sometimes home to as many as a few hundred artists, writers, and performers from over fifty different nations, practising every conceivable art form. I feel privileged to have been selected to come here for a three month residency to write and observe. It has confirmed my faith in the value of multi-culturalism, both its economic value to a nation through cultural tourism, and its human value by creating richness and diversity, which contribute to a nation's racial tolerance. I am also heartened by the great interest shown here by so many people on important social justice issues in Australia, such as Mabo, Wik and the republican debate.

Paris is a few hours by train to London under the English Channel, and all of Europe lies just down the track. This residency has been an ongoing education for me. As I observe and write, I am content just trying to become an improved version of my imperfect self.

All this seems so far away from the Yumba, but this morning, walking along the left bank of the Seine, I discovered yet another type of yumba. Here in the centre of Paris, people are living in cardboard humpies amid the park bushes. (But, as in Germany, colour is not the determining factor for these "yumba dwellers", as it was back home. This time, the homelessness of the underprivileged is the main issue.) Gradually, I have come to realise that outback isolation is a myth, that the yumba back home was not isolated from anywhere else on earth — it was the rest of the world that was isolated from us!

"Paris must inspire you to write" someone remarked the other day. Well, I was inspired years ago sitting in the red

dust under a mulga tree. Paris, like all the other places I
have visited, has broadened my vision and enriched my life
and work, but my inspiration came from elsewhere.

10
GONE BUT NOT FORGOTTEN

SOMETIMES I THINK BACK to when my sister Hazel had trouble describing for that schoolteacher our house in the Yumba. When Hazel was much older she bought a really nice house in the middle of town and sometimes, while she was away, I would be caretaker of this place she called "No Where". It had this name because it quickly became a meeting place (or resting place) for everyone going past. Hazel would always ask people, "Where are you going?" And her friends would usually respond, "Ah, nowhere, Hazel." So my sister had a plaque hung on the gate bearing just that name, "No Where".

"No Where" had many of the things lacking from our home in the Yumba. Many modern appliances and decorations furnished her new home. It always seemed to have a different wall colour whenever I was caretaker, and the furniture was usually in different positions — though them fluffy lace curtains would always be swaying in the breeze.

The bathroom washbasin was bright green and cream and stood beside this big white marble bathtub (oh so different from our old galvanised tub back in the Yumba) which I used to fill with warm running water from the taps above it.

Yet despite all them fittings and interior decorations, I spent most of the stay, as did many of the visitors to "No Where", outside the house under a big open shed beneath the giant gidgee tree. I would then be back to my childhood days spent outdoors, and feel at home again.

Those Yumba days are gone but not forgotten. They are part of my people's history. Now, Murries have their own housing project in the town, brought about by the struggle of so many for equality and a better standard of living.

Over the years individual people have heard our demand for improved living conditions. One local grazier donated a house, which was moved from his station into town in a project assisted by the Girl Guides. Aboriginal families could live in "Jubilee Cottage", as it was called. After five years, the rent they paid would be returned to the family, provided it was put towards buying their own home. Through this inventive scheme quite a few families from the Yumba came to own their own homes. Because most Aboriginal people had only small incomes and few assets they were ineligible to borrow from the bank.

This scheme is no longer in operation although adequate housing is one of our greatest needs. Slowly, but not hopelessly, we are still trying to win the war against discrimination. Dispossession of our land has meant the loss of traditional hunting grounds, which has set us back in our struggle. Since the Dreamtime Aboriginal people have been self-sufficient; land has always been our essential, inherited asset. Without land, the majority of our people are forced to live in poverty, and their children will be

forced to inherit poverty, remaining in complete depend-
ence on white *and black* bureaucracies.

Today, moves towards reconciliation have been made.
And it is now time for all Australian people to start thinking
about our role in helping, even in small ways, to shape the
future and to put behind us resentment stemming from the
past. Maybe we could set an example in doing our bit
towards that ultimate human goal of uniting all the "tribes"
of the world.

Identity was important among the people of the Yumba,
who came from many language groups, living on this small
piece of Crown land in south-west Queensland, supposed
by law to belong to a king living in a palace in England. Yet
every Murri knew this was Kunja land. The land of my mob,
the Kooma people, lay just upstream and stretched east for
miles, taking in parts of the Nebine Creek and Culgoa River.
So we were a diverse mob. There was, for instance, the
so-called "hairless" tribe from the Kooma area. They were
large in build and had lighter skin than us; they looked
eastern Asian in origin. Perhaps they were descended from
Chinese and other sea voyagers who settled in Australia
thousands of years before the Europeans.

The origins of my own existence stretch back beyond
outback Queensland. On Mum's side, her mother was a
Kooma woman with strong Aboriginal beliefs. Granny
Mitchell had been in domestic service on a station near
Dirranbandi when she met her husband, who was head
stockman there. I was never able to find out very much
about Mitchell, though I remember some people describing him as a tall, bearded Irishman, supposed to be associ-
ated with the Kelly Gang. At that time there were many

people, black and white, living in the Nebine Creek area, and my uncles and aunties were not the only ones to know nothing of their father's origins. Granny is supposed to have run away with Mitchell when he moved to work on a station in the Nebine Creek area, where they stayed until his death and where most of my eleven aunties and uncles were born. I never met my grandfather, who died in the 1920s. After his death Granny Mitchell came to live in the Yumba, and I remember her clearly, even though she died when I was very young. She was a stern, no-nonsense old lady. I only back-answered her once, when she gave me a hiding with a green stick. And I recall that when one of my uncles was drowned in the Warrego River and buried in the cemetery close by, after the funeral Granny had all us small kids put inside the house while she smoked out the place, kids and all, cleansing it of any evil spirits that might want to dwell there. She chanted through the whole thing and used special tree branches for this smoking-out ceremony, not the horse and cow manure we used to rid the place of mosquitoes.

Whoever Mitchell was, he was a great father to his dark-skinned kids, protecting them from the law that decreed the removal of children of mixed marriages. My mum and my uncles and aunties often spoke of how this tall white man would look after them whenever a stranger — who might be a feared government person — came to the station. My grandfather would tell the children to go bush, or hide in the humpies of other Aborigines camped close by. Then he would stand at the door of the homestead to greet the unexpected visitor … and on either side of the door would rest a loaded gun in case anyone had any ideas of stealing his dark-skinned children.

My Uncle Natty was was one of the youngest of that clan, and one day his father decided he should have some formal education, so he took him in the sulky to a small township about sixty-five kilometres away to stay with another family that belonged to our mob. Uncle Nat described his week in school there as a week in hell. Being the only Aboriginal boy there he was picked on and bashed by all the white kids. When Mitchell rode back to the town, he found Nat in bed with two black eyes and covered in bruises. The very next day he pulled Nat up onto the horse behind him and took him home to Yunnerman. This ended his formal education. But that school had taught him plenty.

Eventually, after his children had grown up, married and moved away, Mitchell bought a small grazing block in the Nebine Area, where he spent the rest of his life. He left that station to my Uncle Bill, who gave the deeds and Mitchell's will to a policeman for safe keeping. That was the last that was seen or heard of that. Uncle Bill and the rest of the family finished up without any inheritance.

I also remember Uncle Joe, a very tall, dark old man with sharp, fine features. He was Granny Mitchell's brother. Uncle Joe died a few years after Granny, and after his funeral I recall Mum and my Aunty Sissy discussing in hushed tones how to dispose of something Uncle Joe had always carried about with him. I never discovered exactly what it was. But Mum and Aunty Sissy knew that it should not fall into just anyone's hands, because if it was misused it could cause serious damage. As you know, I was someone who always wanted answers. I questioned them about all this, but I hadn't earned the right to receive an answer or know what it was. I listened as they decided they would plant the object in the ground. Later, I thought that it would not be very difficult for me to find its resting place, but I realised that it was better left hidden in Mother Earth. I still wonder about all this, and know that I could have pinpointed the place where that object was buried.

Some claimed that Uncle Joe was a Kadaitcha man, able to conjure up strange events, but to us kids he was simply this ancient old man, tall and straight as a spear made of unbreakable wood. Someone we would never argue with or give cheek to; we sensed that somehow he was different. Without having to say anything he commanded respect. Yet we did not fear him.

As for my father's side of the family, the Whartons, Dad rarely spoke of his parents, and I only ever heard him mention one brother, Tex, who fought in World War I. It was years after Dad died when we learned that he had also come from a large family. He was born at Walgett in New South Wales in 1888, and had six brothers and four sisters. His mother died in 1903, and his father in 1940, in Sydney. Strangely, only two children, Herbert and Barbara, are named on his father's death certificate. Evidently something caused a split in this family.

One day we hope to have a great reunion of the descendants of one Firebrace Wharton, my great-grandfather. He probably married an Aboriginal woman from the Swan Hill area of Victoria, and their son was my grandfather Frederick Horsley Wharton, who married Grace Hendren, born at Manly Beach, New South Wales, in 1856.

It has always been a belief of mine that most European families that have been in Australia for more than four or five generations have some Aboriginal relations. Could this be what caused the split in my father's family — some European family members being unwilling to accept any Aboriginal connection? (Just as, until quite recent times, European Australians were reluctant to accept any convict background in their families.) Anyway, after Grandma Grace died, my father, then a teenager, headed north to the Nebine country in south-west Queensland, where he married my mother and spent the rest of his life working at various jobs while raising their family of nine boys and two girls.

And as for me, for the most part I still live in Cunnamulla. In fifty years I have moved camp from one hundred metres south of the cemetery to one hundred metres north of that white cemetery fence, and one day I'm gonna …

GLOSSARY OF TERMS

belah:	native tree of eastern Australia
bhulan-bhulan:	Murri saying, meaning "might be true — if it wasn't false"
bough-shed:	shed made from four large tree branches acting as posts, with small leafy branches used to make a roof
bugglies:	yabbies, or freshwater crayfish
bumbles:	wild oranges
bungo:	a Murri word for money
coolabah:	a type of eucalypt tree of inland Australia
Condamine bell:	a bell specially crafted on the Condamine Station
corroboree:	an Aboriginal gathering for entertainment or meetings
cuz:	short for cousin, or sometimes friend
Dibble-Dibble:	a mean spirit in Aboriginal mythology
dog tags:	a derogatory term used by Aboriginal people to refer to a certificate entitling them to vote, drink alcohol and exercise the normal rights of Australian citizens
gidgee:	a small native Australian hardwood tree, otherwise known as stinking wattle for the smell it gives off after rain. It is good for firewood

ginjel:	part of a bullock's intestine, considered a real delicacy
goomies:	white or black people who drink methylated spirits or any other alcoholic substances not usually taken
gunghes:	a Murri word for policemen
gungi bal:	a policeman
gunya:	an Aborigine's hut made of bark and tree boughs
Gurra-mutchas:	magical, pigmy-like people of Aboriginal mythology
hopbush:	bright green bush growing on sand with evergreen leaves
humpy:	a bush shelter, similar to a gunya
johnnycake:	a small flat damper of flour cooked on the embers of an open fire
Kadaitcha men:	the lawmen of clans thought to have special powers, often magical
Munta-gutta:	an Aboriginal mythological water spirit, guardian of the waterways
nulla-nulla:	an Aboriginal weapon, similar to a club
pituri:	a bush drug made of ash mixed with the leaves of an Aboriginal intoxicating plant, similar to tobacco
quart pot:	a vessel for holding a quarter of a gallon (1.14 litres) of liquid
shanghai:	a catapult made of a forked stick and elastic
supplejack:	a tree of inland Australia with strong but flexible boughs used for making bows
swag:	a portable mattress for camping
Wham-Boo:	an evil spirit in Aboriginal mythology
wilga:	a small evergreen tree of inland eastern Australia, on which grow delicious edible mistletoe known as "snotty gobble"

willy-willy: a small spiralling wind often gathering
                        dust, rubbish, etc.

withew: a white person

yhudie: a Murri word for totem, which here refers
                        to the family or tribal line, and is a caution
                        against marrying relatives